George Barnett Smith

General Gordon

The Christian soldier and hero

George Barnett Smith

General Gordon
The Christian soldier and hero

ISBN/EAN: 9783337136574

Printed in Europe, USA, Canada, Australia, Japan

Cover: Foto ©Raphael Reischuk / pixelio.de

More available books at **www.hansebooks.com**

GENERAL GORDON

The Christian Soldier and Hero

BY

G. BARNETT SMITH

AUTHOR OF "THE HISTORY OF THE ENGLISH PARLIAMENT;" "JOHN KNOX
AND THE SCOTTISH REFORMATION;" "SIR JOHN FRANKLIN AND THE
ROMANCE OF THE NORTH-WEST PASSAGE," ETC., ETC.

FULLY ILLUSTRATED

LONDON

S. W. PARTRIDGE & CO. LTD.

OLD BAILEY

THE HORSE GUARDS FROM ST. JAMES'S PARK.

PREFACE.

BY the death of CHARLES GEORGE GORDON, England lost one of the best and bravest of her sons. He was well entitled to be styled a modern Bayard, for he closely resembled in many features of his character, "the knight without fear and without reproach." Like him he died with his face to the foe; and like him, his love of virtue, and especially of that kingliest of virtues, justice, was strong and passionate. It is said that Bayard was wont to declare that all empires, kingdoms, and provinces where justice did not rule were mere forests filled with brigands. Could not the same be said of Gordon, who went abroad redressing human wrongs, lifting up the unfortunate and the oppressed and commending the love of that Master whom he served to the whole of the human race? Though always humble in his estimate of himself, no man ever taught more truly by his life the dignity and the grandeur of human nature.

The materials for a biography of Gordon are most abundant, and in the preparation of this brief record of his career, I have been able to draw upon many public sources of information. These include Government papers, Official Despatches, Gordon's own *Journals*, his *Letters* to his Sister, Mr. A. E. Hake's "Story of Chinese Gordon," Wilson's "Ever-Victorious Army," Lilley's "Life and Work of Gordon at Gravesend," Sir Henry W. Gordon's Sketch of his Brother, and the valuable articles published in the *Times*. To all these sources I cordially acknowledge my indebtedness.

There is nothing of a controversial character in the ensuing biography. I have endeavoured to tell briefly the simple but stirring story of Gordon's life from the point of view of the Christian soldier and hero. In his greatness and simplicity, this pure and generous spirit reminds us of Garibaldi, with whom he had much in common. Every member of the Anglo-Saxon race, who studies Gordon's life and character, must feel a thrill of pride that he is of the same blood as this immortal Englishman.

G. B. S.

THE GATE, KHARTOUM.

CONTENTS.

OFF WOOLWICH.

GENERAL GORDON.

CHAPTER I.

GORDON'S BIRTH AND ANCESTRY.

CHARLES GEORGE GORDON, a soldier whose history recalls the career of some noble knight-errant of old, was a native of Woolwich, where he was born on the 28th of January, 1833 There was a fitness in the place of his birth, if we remember merely the military aspect of his character, which was as distinguished as the other features in the life of this strange and many-sided man.

Alike from the traditions of his ancestry, and from the associations of his youth, Gordon seems to have been predestined to an adventurous career. His father, Henry William Gordon, who attained the rank of Lieutenant-General in the Royal Artillery has left behind him an interesting record of his family. From this it appears that Gordon's great grandfather, David Gordon, was taken prisoner at Prestonpans, while serving under Sir John Cope ; his kinsman, Sir William Gordon of Park, fighting in the same engagement under the Pretender. The gallant Highlander was released through the influence of the Duke of Cumberland, who a few years before had stood sponsor to his son, to whom had been given the Duke's name of William Augustus. David Gordon subsequently went to North America, and died at Halifax in 1752. His son, William Augustus, also entered the army, and served with much distinction in various parts of the world. Among other engagements, he was present with Wolfe on the Plains of Abraham in 1759. Returning to England some years later, he was married at Hexham, in Northumberland, in 1773, to Anne Maria Clarke, sister of the Rev. Slaughter Clarke. By this lady he had four daughters and three sons. All the sons entered the army, but two of them died early.

Henry William, the third and only surviving son, was born in 1786, and entered the Royal Artillery. He married Elizabeth, daughter of Mr. Samuel Enderby, of Blackheath, by whom he had eleven children, five sons and six daughters. Charles Gordon was the youngest of these sons. It is stated by Mr. Egmont Hake, one of Gordon's biographers, that our hero's father was "a man of marked individuality. He was a good and complete soldier, with a cultivated

knowledge of his profession. He will be long remembered by those who served under him, as well as
by his family and his friends, for his firm, yet genial
character, and his very striking figure. . . . He lived
by the 'code of honour;' it was the motive of all his
actions, and he expected those with whom he dealt
to be guided by its precepts. It is said that no man
succeeds in his calling unless he considers it the best
and highest. This was General Gordon's feeling for
the army." Again, we are assured that "he was
greatly beloved; for he was kind-hearted, generous,
genial in his nature, always just in his practice and in
his aims. He spent a long life in the service, and,
like his son, was less fitted to obey than to command." Indeed, well as he knew the value of
discipline, he sometimes resisted his superiors, and
protested "against dictates which he would hold to be
superfluous and unjust."

Mrs. Gordon had likewise a remarkable character,
possessing a perfect temper, a cheerful demeanour, an
admirable courage under difficulties, and a genius
for making the best of everything. She came of a
Leicestershire family of merchants and explorers, and,
before the War of Independence, her father traded
much with America, and "took a prominent part in
opening up the resources of the Southern Hemi-
sphere." It was in two of his vessels, chartered by
the British Government, that the historic chests of
tea were carried, which, being thrown overboard in
Boston Harbour, gave the signal for the revolution.

The Enderby Whalers further acquired celebrity in the Southern seas, and were the first to frequent the Pacific round the dangerous Cape Horn. They also made many discoveries in the Antarctic Ocean, including the Falkland Isles, Enderby, and Graham's Lands. Pitt encouraged them in the contraband trade with the western states of South America. In fact, "they were the primary cause of our acquaintance with and settlement of all the important colonies in the Southern Ocean, from Australia to the Fijian-Archipelago."

Young Gordon was educated at Taunton, and at one period of his youth he had for his companion and mentor his elder brother, Major-General Enderby Gordon. When he was a little more than fifteen years of age, however, he was entered at the Royal Military Academy at Woolwich. For the mere acquisition of facts or rules Gordon had never any taste ; he was not cut out after the ordinary pattern ; and even the drudgery necessary to obtain admission into the ranks of the senior arm of the service was distasteful to him. Once he was severely rebuked, and told that "he would never make an officer." The rebuke does not seem to have been altogether merited, and the spirited cadet, who felt it keenly, "tore his epaulets from his shoulders, and cast them at his superior's feet."

But the erratic military student passed his examinations successfully, and obtained his commission in the Royal Engineers. Stationed first at Pembroke

Dock, in 1854, he was employed in connection with the fortifications then being erected for the protection of the new docks. But his thoughts were deeply occupied with the important events then transpiring in the Crimea. As regards his early military experiences, his letters demonstrate that from the first day of his entrance into the army he took a keen interest

THE SCHOOL AT TAUNTON WHERE GORDON WAS EDUCATED.

in all that concerned his profession, and that he zealously applied himself to the mastery of all its technical details.

A great longing came over him to be sent out to the seat of war in the Crimea, and he dreaded being drafted instead to the West Indies or to New Zealand. Much to his satisfaction, in December, 1854—when it was seen that the Allied Forces must spend the winter before Sebastopol — he received orders to proceed with some huts to the Crimea. He secured a variation in the order by obtaining permission to travel himself overland to Marseilles, while the huts were sent round by sea in a collier.

It is in the East, therefore, that the curtain rises upon the first act in his strange and fateful career, just as it was in the East that it descended upon the last, sad, and tragic scene of his eventful history.

IN THE TRENCHES.

CHAPTER II.

SERVICES IN THE CRIMEA AND ARMENIA.

GORDON arrived at Balaclava, his destination in the Crimea, in January, 1855. The familiar story of the breakdown of the British commissariat was emphasised by the young soldier in his letters home. For some weeks he was not appointed to active service, and he had, therefore, an opportunity for closely observing the condition of the troops, and the position of the allied forces.

At length he was detailed for duty in the trenches before Sebastopol. He seems thus early to have borne a charmed life, for he describes how he was first fired upon in mistake by the English sentries, then by the Russian pickets; yet after the working party and sentries under his command had bolted, he succeeded in carrying out his first definite order. He had been instructed to effect a junction by means of rifle-pits, between the French and English sentries, who were stationed in advance of the trenches.

From the 28th of February to the 9th of April, he was engaged in making new batteries in the advance trenches. Once he had a very narrow escape. A Russian bullet passed within an inch of his head, but his only comment upon the incident in writing home was, " They (the Russians) are very good marksmen ; their bullet is large and pointed."

Another anecdote will sufficiently show Gordon's heroic spirit. In going round the trenches one day he heard a corporal and a sapper of engineers in a violent altercation. Stopping to ask what was the matter, he was told that the men were engaged placing some fresh gabions in the battery, and that the corporal had ordered the sapper to stand up on the parapet, where he was exposed to the enemy's fire, while the officer, in full shelter of the battery, handed the baskets up to him. Gordon jumped upon the parapet, and ordered the corporal to join him, while the sapper handed them the gabions. After the work was done, and done under the fire of the watchful Russian gunners, Gordon turned to the corporal and said, " Never order a man to do anything that you are afraid to do yourself."

Heavy firing was resumed on the 9th of April, and it continued for some weeks. The British suffered severe losses in the trenches, especially among the

officers.   Yet Gordon remained unscathed, although
he courted danger and was actively engaged the whole
time.   He was present at numerous sorties in front of
the Redan, and on one occasion several officers and
seventy men were killed and wounded.   He did not
think much of the courage of the French, but he
regarded the Russians as splendidly brave, though he
subsequently had reason to modify this opinion.   In
June the whole of the batteries on both sides were
engaged, and the casualties were very great.   Gordon
was in the trenches the whole time, and was slightly
wounded, but he continued his work.   The French
attacked the Mamelon, and this and various redoubts
were captured.   The English meantime secured the
quarries.   Gordon's brother, writing home, said :
" Only a few lines to say Charley is all right, and has
escaped amidst a terrific shower of grape and shells
of every description.   You may imagine the suspense
I was kept in until assured of his safety.   He cannot
write himself, and is now fast asleep in his tent,
having been in the trenches from two o'clock yesterday morning, during the cannonade, until seven last
night, and again from 12.30 this morning until noon."

The siege of Sebastopol went on for some months
after this, and the lack of energy and activity was
very irritating to the restless mind of Gordon.   At
last, however, on the 8th of September, the French
captured the Malakoff, and the English made a
desperate but unsuccessful assault upon the Redan.
It was then decided that the Highlanders should

B

storm the Redan, but before this operation could be
carried out, the Russians evacuated Sebastopol.
Gordon, in describing what he witnessed at daybreak
on the 9th, wrote: "During the night of the 8th I
heard terrific explosions, and on going down to the
trenches at four the next morning, I saw a splendid
sight. The whole of Sebastopol was in flames, and
every now and then terrible explosions took place,
while the rising sun shining on the place had a most
beautiful effect. The Russians were leaving the town
by the bridge; all the three-deckers were sunk, the
steamers alone remaining. Tons and tons of powder
must have been blown up. About eight o'clock I got
an order to commence a plan of the works, for which
purpose I went to the Redan, where a dreadful sight
was presented. The dead were buried in the ditch—
the Russians with the English—Mr. Wright reading
the burial service over them."

The English troops entered the southern portion
of the town of Sebastopol on the evening of the 10th,
and Gordon was entrusted with a responsible share in
the work of destroying the harbour and fortifications
upon which successive Czars had bestowed an expenditure of millions sterling. He likewise took part in
the siege and capture of the fortress of Kinburn.
Those competent to judge have noted how the young
engineer at this period revealed the qualities which
most characterised his later and more famous
achievements in Asia and Africa. His actions were
not merely distinguished for a natural simplicity and

steadfast devotion to duty, but they also evinced military skill, and that extraordinary fascination he was able to exercise over all men with whom he was brought into contact. Colonel Chesney bore testimony that in the trench work before Sebastopol,

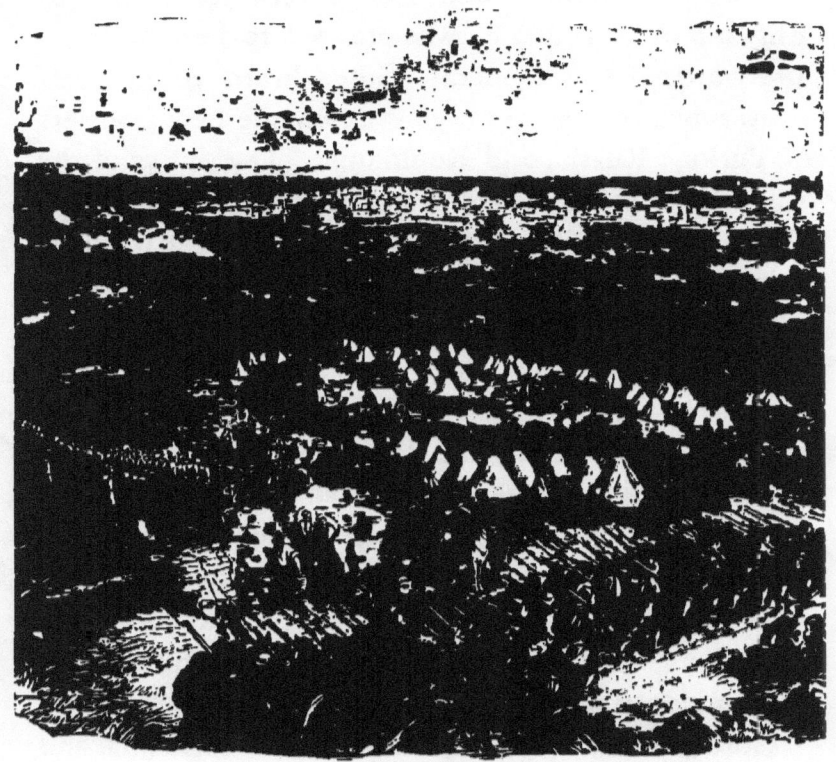

SEBASTOPOL.

Gordon acquired a personal knowledge of the enemy's movements such as no other officer attained. Indeed, he was generally sent to find out what new move the Russians were making. Owing to the operation of the seniority principle in his corps he could not be promoted, but he was decorated with the Legion of Honour—an unusual distinction for a youth of twenty-three.

The Crimean War did not end Gordon's experiences among the Russians. When the majority of the English officers and troops returned either to England or to India, he was ordered to join Major— afterwards Lieut.-General—Sir Edward Stanton, in Bessarabia, to assist in laying down the new frontiers of Turkey, Russia, and Roumania. The duties of the English Commissioners were to trace a boundary about 100 miles in length, and to compare it with the Russian maps ; but so many disputes arose between the representatives of the various nations interested, that eleven months were consumed in the task. Gordon was greatly interested in his work, and visited many Eastern cities ; and the experience he gained in this capacity was deemed so useful in official quarters, that he was soon told off for similar work. In April, 1857, he was instructed to join Colonel— afterwards General—Sir Lintorn Simmons, in the important work connected with the delimitation of the boundary in Asia.

Gordon was engaged for some time in Armenia, and visited Erzeroum, Kars, Erivan, and other places. He also ascended Little and Great Ararat, with the object of personally ascertaining their respective heights. The closer experience he now gained of the Russians did not impress him at all favourably. He had, likewise, his first experience of uncivilised tribes, over whom in the future he was to exercise such a dominant sway. Summoned after a stay of six months in these distant regions to a Conference of the Commission at Constantinople, he was detained for some time in the Turkish capital in consequence of the illness of his chief.

Then he was permitted to return to England on a welcome visit. He had been away for three years, and after a rest of six months, he was once more sent out as Commissioner to Armenia. For the greater part of the year 1858, he was engaged in verifying the frontier newly laid down, and in examining the new road between the Russian and Turkish dominions.

Although the religious convictions of Gordon at this time do not assume great prominence, we find from his letters that he had taken his first sacrament on Easter Day, 1854, and had continued frequently to commune afterwards. There are also evidences that he was already swayed by that belief in fate or destiny which came afterwards to exercise so strong an influence over him.

A capable critic of Gordon's career, writing in the *Times* after his death concerning this early period, observed :—" His letters show him to have been a very intelligent and a very assiduous officer in his profession, with the true military instinct, and a skill in draughtsmanship not often surpassed. At the same time, there are many indications that the writer was even at the early age to which we refer something more than serious, and a skilful analyser of the human mind might have declared that his original religious belief would, under the precise circumstances of his later wonder-working career in China and the Soudan, have produced exactly such a state of religious conviction as Gordon had attained during the last fifteen or sixteen years of his life. But in these early days, the young engineer kept his opinions on these matters of supreme importance to himself, and even in his confidential and private letters there is only a casual reference to the subject. The letters are full, however, of military knowledge and enthusiasm, and reveal the caution, the energy, and the thoroughness in regard to details which, when combined with the high moral qualities needed for the assertion of European superiority over Asiatics, enabled him in China to achieve some of the most remarkable military triumphs that are recorded in history."

After his second return from Armenia, Gordon was stationed at Chatham for a short period, where he was engaged as Field-work Instructor and Adjutant.

PKKIN.

CHAPTER III.

HIS CAREER IN CHINA.

IN July, 1860, Gordon left England for China, where an Anglo-French expedition was carrying on operations to compel the Chinese to ratify the treaty concluded by Lord Elgin in the previous year, and also to exact reparation for the attack on Admiral Hope's squadron by the garrison of the Taku Forts.

On arriving at Tientsin towards the close of September, he learned that Sir Harry Parkes, together with his companions and escort, had been treacherously captured and ill-treated. As the result of this outrage, the Allies marched on Pekin in October, and invested the capital. Gordon took part in the advance on Pekin, in the battle of Chan Chia Wan, and in the subsequent destruction of the Summer Palace.

Writing home a graphic description of the destruction of this remarkable Palace, Gordon observed :— "The General ordered it to be destroyed, and stuck up proclamations to say why it was so ordered. We accordingly went out, and after pillaging it, burned the whole place, destroying in a vandal-like manner most valuable property, which could not be replaced for four millions. We got upwards of £48 a-piece prize money before we went out from here; and although I have not as much as many, I have done well. Imagine D. giving sixteen shillings for a string of pearls which he sold the next day for £500. The people are civil, but I think the grandees hate us, as they must after what we did to the palace. You can scarcely imagine the beauty and magnificence of the places we burnt. It made one's heart sore to burn them ; in fact, these palaces were so large, and we were so pressed for time, that we could not plunder them carefully. Quantities of gold ornaments were burned, considered as brass. It was wretchedly demoralising work for an army. Everybody was wild for plunder.

"You could scarcely conceive the magnificence of the Summer Palace, or the tremendous devastation the French have committed. The throne and throne-room were lined with ebony, carved in a marvellous way. There were huge mirrors of all shapes and kinds, clocks, watches, musical boxes with puppets on them, magnificent china of every description, heaps and heaps of silks of all colours, embroidery, and as much splendour and civilisation as you would see at Windsor; carved ivory screens, coral screens, large amounts of treasure, etc. The French have smashed everything in the most wanton way. It was a scene of utter destruction which passes my description."

A treaty of peace having been signed, Gordon, as Commanding Engineer, was stationed with his regiment at Tientsin, which was to remain occupied by an English force pending the final arrangements for the establishment of the English and other foreign Ministers in Pekin itself. The young English officer, who could never remain idle, employed his leisure in surveying the country round Tientsin, and in mapping the road along the banks of the Peiho to the Taku Forts. On one occasion he rode with his friend, Lieut. Cardew, to Kalgan, one of the principal towns and gates of the Great Wall, through a part of China then entirely unknown to Europeans. The travellers conveyed their luggage in two of the lumbering native carts, which had no springs, and whose large wooden wheels were only adaptable to the deep ruts of certain parts of the province. On leaving that part of the province in which the carts had been made, the axles had to be widened, in order to suit the broader ruts. A Chinese boy acted as interpreter, and the adventurous journey did not end without its exciting incident. At Taiyuen, which has been described as the Toledo of China on account of the superiority of its cutlery, they had serious

trouble with an innkeeper, who charged an extortionate
sum for the night's lodging and meagre fare that he
had provided. As expostulation made no impression, and a threatening crowd assembled, Captain
Gordon devised a clever expedient. Ordering the
boy and his carts to hasten, as fast as possible, along
the road to Pekin, he covered the most demonstrative
of the crowd with his revolver. This being wrested
from him, however, he called out, " Let us go to the
Yamên, and settle the matter before the Mandarin."
With this the crowd became pacified, and the
revolver was returned. The whole party then proceeded to the Yamên, but when they reached the
door, Gordon gave his comrade a signal, and they
both turned their horses' heads and galloped off as
fast as they could, followed in close pursuit by the
mob. They succeeded in getting rid of their pursuers,
and in reaching Tientsin in safety, although not
without several incidents of a similar character.

For nearly two years Gordon remained in Northern
China, and then, in May, 1862, he was summoned to
the coast of Central China, which had become the
theatre of the most important events then happening
in that empire. The depredations of the Tai-ping
rebels in the neighbourhood of Shanghai compelled
the English commander, Sir Charles Staveley, to take
steps for clearing the district of these marauding
bands. Gordon was given the command of the
Engineers against the rebels, and with his men he
stormed and entered Singpoo, and subsequently

drove the enemy from other strongholds. After severe fighting, and with some British loss, the followers of T'ien Wang, the insurgent leader, were driven from all the towns which they had seized within a radius of thirty miles of Shanghai. The English policy then reverted to one of strict neutrality between the Chinese Government and the rebels.

But Gordon himself was still actively employed, for as Engineer officer he had to make a thorough survey of the region which had just been cleared of the Tai-pings. It was while engaged in this onerous task that he acquired his intimate knowledge of the country and the people. He not only perceived the hollowness of the Tai-ping pretensions, but became perfectly convinced of the futility of their efforts; and his sympathy being enlisted on behalf of the unfortunate country people who suffered so much through the rising, he earnestly desired a speedy termination to the disastrous Civil War.

The Tai-ping rebellion, however, was as yet by no means crushed, and in order that the reader may understand its origin and aims, we will briefly trace its course from its inception in 1851. Foreigners gave the name of Tai-pings to the followers of the leader of the revolt, Hung Hsia-ch'wan, who raised the standard of insurrection in the year just named. Hung was born in 1813, in a poor agricultural village in the province of Canton. He was a diligent student in his youth, but he failed in his academical competitions. In 1837 he fell into an illness, during which he saw visions, and conceived the idea of changing the religion of the empire, as well as overthrowing the ruling Manchâu dynasty. Gradually making converts to his views, in 1844 he went into the adjoining province of Kiangsu, where he formed communities called " Churches of God." He also issued revelations communicated to him by " The Heavenly Father," and the " Heavenly Elder Brother " Christ. Rules of conduct and organisation were promulgated, and after several years the insurgents found themselves sufficiently strong to take possession of the district city of Yung-au. The leader was now hailed as emperor of the dynasty of Tai-ping, or Grand Peace ; and T'ien Kwo, or Kingdom of Heaven, was adopted as the name of his reign. Hung himself was styled T'ien Wang, or the Heavenly King, and he gave to a number of his lieutenants the title of Wang, or king. Although besieged in April, 1852, by the Imperialists, the rebels broke through the ranks of their foes, and marched northwards.

After various other successes, they captured the important city of Nanking in March, 1853, putting the whole of the Manchâu garrison to the sword. The number of the rebels was now calculated at 100,000. The Tai-ping dynasty was proclaimed anew, and fealty sworn to the Heavenly King. The leader despatched a large force for the capture of Pekin, as the crowning triumph of the movement. The expedition made considerable progress, but not being supported by reinforcements, the leaders were compelled to retreat towards Nanking in 1855. Dissensions now arose between the rival kings, and Hung lost much of his power. His promise of Christian institutions had not been fulfilled, and he

THE VICEROY LI.

was unable to establish a firm government in the revolted provinces.

New kings were appointed, and some of these proved to be men of great ability, who subdued important capitals like Sû-châu and Nang-châu. Unable adequately to cope with the insurrection, the Imperialists called in the assistance of foreigners. A body of men of different nationalities entered their service under the command of an American named General Ward. This body did good service until its leader was killed in 1862. It was styled the Ever-Victorious Army, but this title was not justified until Gordon assumed the command of it, as we shall see, and earned for himself the designation of Chinese Gordon—a name by which he was ever afterwards distinguished.

Burgevine, Ward's successor, having been disgraced and dismissed from the service for an act of violence, and two other leaders, Holland and Tapp, having been discredited by reverses in the field, the Governor-General of the Kiang Provinces, Li-Hung-Chang—since known to European fame as the celebrated statesman—appealed to General Staveley to appoint an English officer, in whom he had confidence, for the command of the foreign drilled force. Although he would have control also over Imperialist troops, it was the foreign element under his command which the Chinese authorities mainly relied upon to subjugate the rebels.

General Staveley at once nominated Gordon for this honourable, but very difficult service, and the appointment was referred to the Horse Guards, whose sanction was necessary. This was given in due course, and Gordon, to whom was awarded the brevet rank of major, took the field in connection with this new enterprise on the 24th of March, 1863.

A CHINESE RIVER-BOAT.

CHAPTER IV.

CAREER IN CHINA—*(continued)*.

THE fortunes of the Imperialists were not very flourishing when Gordon assumed the command of the Ever-Victorious Army. Although on the great river, Yang-tse-kiang, the Tai-pings held little more than Nanking, while the forces of the Government had somewhat increased in numbers and efficiency, there was still grave cause for disquietude. In the important districts of Kiangsu and on the route of the Grand Canal, the efforts of Chung Wang, the ablest of the Tai-ping leaders, had been crowned with success; and the Imperialists, afraid to encounter his forces in the open field, surrendered most of the few towns in their possession on the demand of the rebels.

Not only was Gordon thus faced by an enemy rendered bold and confident by success, but he had to contend against insubordination in his own troops, and jealousy on the part of his Chinese colleagues. One who was thoroughly acquainted with his position and difficulties at this period, thus wrote concerning them :—

"It would have been unreasonable to suppose that the appointment of a young English Engineer officer to the command of a force, which, it was considered, would more probably disobey him than accept him as its leader, could suffice to restore the doubtful fortune of a war that had already continued for two years, under very similar conditions. Yet, clearly the whole result depended on whether he would succeed better than Ward, or Burgevine, or Holland, in vanquishing the more desperate and well-armed rebels who were in actual possession of all the strong places in the province of Kiangsu, and whose detachments stretched from Hang-chow to Nanking. There was also another danger — the disciplined Chinese contingent, now numbering five regiments, with their foreign officers, of all nationalities—adventurers, unrestrained by any consideration of obedience to their own governments —furnished the means of great mischief should any leader present himself to exhort them to fight for their own hand, and to carve out a dominion for themselves. The possibility was far from chimerical ; it was fully realised and appreciated by the English authorities. A great responsibility, therefore, devolved upon Major Gordon. He had not merely to beat a victorious enemy, and to restore the confidence and discipline of his defeated troops, but he had also to advance the objects of the English Government, and to redeem the rights of a long-outraged people. Unlike his predecessors, he had no personal aims for himself ; he did not wish to displace or weaken the authority of the Chinese officials, and his paramount thought was how to rescue the unfortunate inhabitants of Kiangsu from the calamities which had desolated their hearths, and driven whole towns and districts to the verge of destruction and despair."

Gordon's campaign began with the re-capture of Fushan, a small fortified town on the coast, north of Shanghai. As one of the results of this success, the Tai-pings retired from the blockade of Chanza, thus permitting one of the few remaining Imperial garrisons to recover its communication with the outer world. But against this was to be set the loss of 1500 Chinese troops, who had been led into an ambuscade at Taitsan, under the pretence of a desire on the part of the garrison to surrender. This disaster was especially galling to Li-Hung-Chang, as Taitsan had already witnessed more than one Imperialist defeat, and he therefore urged Major Gordon to at once retrieve the loss. Accordingly, on the 1st of May, 1863, Gordon attacked Taitsan with great energy, and the fighting lasted for two days. The Tai-pings fought courageously and stubbornly, and the result still hung in the balance when Gordon received valuable assistance from two howitzers, which opportunely arrived. This proved the turning point of the struggle, and the rebels were at last compelled to desert the ramparts and evacuate the town.

Quinsan was the next place, and perhaps the most important of all, invested by Gordon. It was a strong and commanding position, situated on a creek leading into the Grand Canal at Soochow. "Not only would its possession enable Gordon to hold the conquests he had already effected ; it was also the key to Soochow, which, once reduced, would restore the eastern half of the rebel territory to the Imperial Government." But just when Gordon was preparing for the assault, he was again met by insubordination in his troops. Having appointed an officer named Cooksley over the commissariat and military stores, with the rank of lieutenant-colonel, the native majors demanded from their commander the same rank and pay as the newly-appointed colonel. Gordon refused this, where-upon the officers tendered their resignations, but requested to be allowed to serve on the impending expedition. Gordon accepted the resignations, but declined the offers of service.

At length the recalcitrant officers were compelled to make their submission, and Gordon set forth with 600 artillery and 2300 infantry to the attack of Quinsan. The enemy numbered some 12,000, most of whom were strongly entrenched. Nevertheless, Gordon pressed forward, but as an attack in front would have entailed heavy loss, and might have proved unsuccessful, he first attacked the stockades on the right flank, and carried them. Next, he reconnoitred the rear of the town from a steamer upon which he succeeded in making his way for a considerable distance up the creek towards Soochow This examination of their line of retreat alarmed the rebels, who fled precipitately the moment they discovered that Gordon, in the steamer *Hyson*, had carried the stockades at Chunye, a short distance west of Quinsan itself. By one of the boldest and most successful feats of daring, Gordon thus captured the key-stone position of Quinsan, which now became his headquarters, as well as a base for the realisation of his ultimate object, the reduction of Soochow.

Unfounded charges of cruelty towards the rebels obtained currency at this time. They arose out of the execution by the Imperialists of seven prisoners who were special offenders, and who had been guilty of the act of bloody treachery which sacrificed the lives of half the Chinese column entrapped in Taitsan. It was claimed that they had no right to be treated as prisoners of war. One styling himself "An Eye Witness" informed the Bishop of Victoria that the seven men had been done to death by tortures exhibiting the most refined cruelty; and the Bishop communicated with Lord John Russell, the British Foreign Secretary. There was no truth in this exaggerated story, but it was followed up by other false reports of "unmentionable atrocities," which worked some harm to Gordon's position and the cause he had espoused. Writing on this subject to the *Shanghai Shipping News*, under date 15th of June, 1863, Gordon said —

"I am of belief that the Chinese of this force are quite as merciful in action as the soldiers of any Christian nation could be; and, in proof of this, can point to over 700 prisoners, taken in the last engagement (Quinsan), who are now in our employ. Some have entered our ranks, and done service against the rebels since their capture. But one life has been taken out of this number, and that one was a rebel who tried to induce his comrades to fall on the guard, and who was shot on the spot. It is a great mistake to imagine that the men of this force are worthless. They will, in the heat of action, put their enemies to death, as the troops of any nation would do; but when the fight is over, they will associate as freely together as if they had never fought. If 'Observer' and 'Eye-witness,' with their friend 'Justice and Mercy,' would come forward and communicate what they know, it would be far more satisfactory than writing statements of the nature of those alluded to by the Bishop of Victoria. And if any one is under the impression that the inhabitants of the rebel districts like their masters, he has only to come up here to be disabused of his idea. I do not exaggerate when I say that upwards of 1500 rebels were killed in their retreat from Quinsan by the villagers, who rose *en masse*."

Gordon himself was most scrupulous in his own conduct of the war. When his soldiers at Taitsan were guilty of plunder, contrary to his articles of war, they were punished by being marched off to the siege of Quinsan before opportunity was afforded them of selling their loot.

The great work of reducing Soochow did not actually begin until September. Writing to a military friend touching the strength and condition of his troops, Gordon said :—" I hope you do not think that I have a magnificent army. You never did see such a rabble as it was, and, although I think I have improved it, it is still sadly wanting. I now occupy a most commanding position with respect to the rebels, being able to attack them along a very wide front; but then they have nearly 50,000 men in Soochow, and I have 3000, and three steamers. Now both officers and men, although ragged and perhaps slightly disreputable, are in capital order, and well disposed. Some of the prisoners are in my body-guard, and want to fight their old friends." In another letter, he observed with regard to himself: " The Governor of the Province, Prince Kung, and nearly all the Mandarins, are satisfied with my appointment. I rejoice in the rank of Tsung-Ping, or Red Button Mandarin, but I do not wear the dress, as you may suppose. They write me very handsome letters, and are very civil in every way. I like them, but they require a great deal of tact, and getting in a rage with their apathy is detrimental, so I put up with it."

On one occasion, when an alarming mutiny broke out among his troops, Gordon was obliged to act with a severity which greatly pained him, though it was absolutely necessary. Mr. Egmont Hake thus describes the incident :—

"The artillery refused to fall in, and threatened to blow the officers to pieces, both European and Chinese. The intimation of this serious mutiny was conveyed to Gordon in a written proclamation, and he at once took measures that showed it was no easy task to shake him in his absolute command. Convinced that the non-commissioned officers were at the bottom of the affair, he called them up and asked who wrote the proclamation and why the men would not fall in. They had not the courage to tell the truth, and professed ignorance on both points. With quiet determination Gordon then told them that one in every five would be shot, an announcement which they received with groans. During this manifestation, the Commander, with great shrewdness, determined in his own mind that the man whose groans were the most prolonged and emphatic, was the ringleader. This man was a corporal : Gordon approached him, dragged him out of the rank with his own hand, and ordered two of the infantry standing by to shoot him on the spot. The order was instantly obeyed. Gordon then sent the remaining non-commissioned officers into confinement for one hour, with the assurance that within that time if the men did not fall in, and if the name of the writer of the proclamation was not given up, every fifth man among them would be shot. This brought them to their senses. The files fell in ; the writer's name

"GORDON DRAGGED HIM OUT OF THE RANK."

was disclosed. Gordon had done justice to him some hours before ; it was the loud-voiced corporal."

Several preliminary skirmishes took place before the siege of Soochow, in which Gordon was uniformly successful, but a difficulty of no light character arose when Burgevine—who, as already stated, previously commanded the Imperialists — joined the armies of the rebel sovereign, and became a Wang. The knowledge of this unsettled some of Gordon's men, who admired Burgevine's system of plunder and his desperate methods. Then, some of the artillery officers refused to serve under Major Tapp, a new leader selected by the Commander. Gordon's firmness, nevertheless, carried him through, as it had done on many previous occasions. Governor Li, with whom also he had many differences, soon came to recognise Gordon's sterling qualities and military genius, and became his warm and devoted friend.

At one time Gordon was so disgusted with the apathy and opposition of his Chinese colleagues, that he resigned the leadership of the army, and it was only the news of Burgevine's secession to the rebels which induced him to withdraw his resignation, and to push forward with the siege of Soochow. After a time, when Burgevine began to see that he would not be able to contend against Gordon, he requested an interview with him, in the course of which he broached an extraordinary scheme. It was no less than that Gordon should join him, and that they should found a Chinese Empire for themselves. Burgevine suggested that they should seize upon Soochow, expel both rebels and Imperialists, lay hands on the treasure contained therein, raise an army of 20,000 men, and march on Pekin. Gordon indignantly and contemptuously rejected these overtures, and informed Burgevine that it would be better and wiser to confine his attention to whether he intended to surrender or not, instead of discussing impossible schemes of personal ambition.

A writer in the *Times* described the siege and capture of Soochow as "the greatest and most difficult of Gordon's exploits in China." Having established himself securely on both the eastern and southern sides of the town, the Commander took steps to shut the Tai-pings in on the western side also. This he accomplished ; and then, after a desperate battle at Laeku, where an officer was killed at his side, he acquired a position to the north of the town as well. What followed is thus related by the writer just quoted :—"By the middle of October, Major Gordon had, with a force of less than 15,000 men, almost succeeded in completely investing the Tai-ping army of 40,000 men which garrisoned Soochow, and it became his chief care to perfect the investment on the north by the capture of Fusaiquan, the last of the Tai-ping positions, which gave them the command of the navigation of the Grand Canal. Through the treachery or incapacity of the commander, the resistance encountered was insignificant, and Major Gordon had the satisfaction of completing the investment of

Soochow at a very slight loss in comparison with the
result achieved.   On the 27th of November Major
Gordon opened his first attack on the main defences
of Soochow by a night assault upon the Low Mun
stockades, in front of the East Gate.   For the first,
but not, unfortunately, for the last time, he was to
experience the inconstancy of fortune.   The Tai-pings
had been warned of the coming foe, and in the dark
the attacking force became disordered.   After a
desperate effort to retrieve matters, Major Gordon
drew off his force, with a loss of about 165 killed and
wounded.   Nothing dismayed, Major Gordon con-
centrated the whole of his force for a fresh attack,
and, after a heavy cannonade, he carried the Low
Mun stockades at the head of his men.   It is appro-
priate to state here that, although he had to organise
the simplest details in person, Major Gordon was
always the first man in these attacks.   It was he who
showed the way to victory as well as how to prepare
for it ; but he never carried any weapon save a small
cane, which the Chinese soon regarded with almost
superstitious reverence, and named his 'wand of
victory.'

" The capture of the Low Mun stockades practically entailed the fall of Soochow itself.   Chung Wang,
who in the worst extremity never despaired, abandoned it to its fate, and the Wangs, or chiefs, who
remained, turned their attention, not to prolonging
the defence, but to obtaining the best possible terms
from the Chinese authorities.   Major Gordon was, of

course, in favour of according the most lenient conditions to a brave enemy, and, indeed, there were the strongest reasons for not driving to desperation the large number of men in Soochow, who still far exceeded the force by which they were hemmed in. Several interviews were held between Gordon and Li-Hung-Chang on the one side, and Moh-Wang and his lieutenants on the other; and as the result of these negotiations the garrison was admitted to terms and the Tai-ping leaders were promised their lives."

The nature of this bold exploit of the investment and capture of Soochow may be gathered from the numbers employed on both sides. The Imperialists had from 13,000 to 14,000 men, of whom between 3000 and 4000 were under Gordon's orders. There were, too, in the neighbourhood 25,000 Imperialists besides, whose centre was at Fushan, and who were under General Ching. The Tai-pings had 40,000 men at Soochow and the suburbs alone, with 20,000 more in the city of Wusieh, and 18,000 in Mahtanchiao, a place between Wusieh and Soochow, whence Chung Wang, the Faithful King, could attack on the flank any advance on the Grand Canal. Notwithstanding these heavy odds, Gordon conquered brilliantly.

With regard to the rebel kings, Gordon held himself pledged personally for the safety of Moh-Wang, for whom he entertained a genuine esteem, and who had spared the life of Burgevine when the latter had been detected in dastardly and treacherous acts. The English commander was consequently filled with dismay when he discovered that tne Chinese leaders had consummated a deed of treachery by putting the rebel kings to death. In his eyes nothing whatever could be pleaded in extenuation of such an act. It was only by the merest accident that Gordon discovered that the Wangs had been foully murdered; and when he hastened into the city to discover the full extent of the breach of faith which had been committed, and to exact summary vengeance on those who had perpetrated it, and thereby sullied his own good faith, he nearly fell a victim himself to the angry Tai-pings. His peril at this time Mr. Hake thus indicates:—"So ill-organised was the local Chinese Government, and so independent was Li of the military commanders, to whom he owed the supremacy he enjoyed, that he not only executed his own plans without reference to others, but did not even intimate to Gordon—who was, he may possibly have believed, in quarters at Quinsan—the danger of entering the city. By this time he had beheaded the principal Wangs, and given up Soochow to plunder. Gordon's situation was most perilous; what made it worse was that he was wholly ignorant of the massacre which had been secretly effected outside the town, and of which Ching had not had the courage to inform him. It is not surprising, therefore, that when he entered the courtyard of the house with Nar-Wang's uncle and his family, he at once was surrounded by some thousands of armed Tai-pings, who shut the gates on him as he went in, and declined to allow him to send out his interpreter with a message to his troops. Fortunately, it happened that the Tai-pings no more knew than Gordon himself that their chiefs had been put to death. Had they done so, they would have held Gordon responsible, and might have put him to torture. As it was, they held him as a hostage for the good treatment of their leaders. He was kept powerless in the palace from the afternoon of the 6th till the morning of the next day, surrounded by Tai-pings, who knew that the city was being plundered contrary to treaty, and who must have surmised that bloodshed was going on, and that some untoward fate had overtaken the Wangs who had gone out to Governor Li. Such a suspicion might have made Gordon their victim ; but he was left unharmed, probably from the forlorn hope that his presence might yet be a protection to themselves. Few men have looked upon death under circum-stances so intricate and so threatening. But Gordon's life was to be preserved for other times and other events."

It was not to be supposed that a man like Gordon would rest until he had ascertained what had become of the Wangs. Accordingly, we read that " by two in the morning he had prevailed on his captors to let his interpreter take a letter out to his boat, which lay at anchor under the South Gate. It is characteristic of him that his message contained no reference to himself, but consisted of an order to the captain of his flotilla to seize on the Governor's person, and lay him by the heels until the Wangs were given up. This was a fine stroke of policy and perfectly sincere ; but it failed. The guide in charge returned alone, stating that the interpreter had been seized by the Imperialists, and the letter taken and torn up. At three o'clock the Tai-pings were so far persuaded as to allow Gordon himself to go out in search of the missing interpreter. He reached the South Gate, where some Imperialist soldiers, not knowing probably who he was, took him prisoner for being in the company of rebels. From them he made his escape, and found his way round to the East Gate, where his body-guard was camped under Major Brookes. True to his purpose and to his word, he sent the guard at once to the protection of the Tai-pings he had quitted an hour before. Soon after, General Ching made his appearance ; but Gordon, after all that had happened to himself, and all that he had witnessed in the city, refused to hold communication with him. Ching then sent an artillery officer named Bailey to explain matters. But this gentleman had not the courage to tell the truth ; and when Gordon asked him what had become of the Wangs, and if they were still prisoners, he replied that he did not know, but that he would bring in Nar-Wang's son, who was in his tent.

"The interview which followed opened Gordon's eyes. He learned that the Wangs had been executed on the previous day, and was so deeply moved by the intelligence that he burst into tears. He at once crossed the creek, on the other bank of which the Wangs had been murdered, and there he was not long in discovering their bodies, headless and frightfully gashed.

" It was, probably, the most trying moment of his life, and never perhaps had he before given way to so angry an outburst of sorrow.   Not only was this treachery needless and brutal, but the feeling came bitterly home to him that his own honour was at stake.   He had pledged himself for their safety, but he had negotiated with them on the understanding, as a primary condition, that their lives would be spared.   As we have seen, he had refused to hold any parley with Ching.   That General, however, had seen enough of his state of mind to greatly fear the consequences, and to feel that the Governor's life was in danger should Gordon come in contact with him. Not the least offence to Gordon—a very flagrant one in itself—was that the Imperialists had sacked the city.   Owing to this discourtesy, the man, through whose daring and skill Soochow had fallen, saw himself made a prisoner and in peril of his life.   It is not to be wondered at if Gordon was enraged beyond bounds, and it is not surprising that, for the first time during the war, he armed himself and went out to seek the life of an enemy.   He took a revolver and sought the Governor's quarters, fully resolved to do justice on his body, and accept the consequences.

" But Ching was on the alert.   He was scared at the terrible form of Gordon's anger, and contrived to give the Governor the alarm. Gordon boarded his boat, only to find that Li had taken refuge in the plundered city. Thither he hastened in pursuit. Li, however, went into hiding, and, though Gordon was 'hot and instant in his 'race' for many days, he never came up with him. He had ordered up his troops to assist him in running the fugitive to earth ; but when he found his efforts were in vain, he marched them back into quarters at Quinsan. There, with the deepest emotion, he read them an account of what had happened. He intimated to his officers that it was impossible for a British soldier to serve any longer under Governor Li ; that he did not purpose to disband his force, but that he should hand it over to General Brown, the commander of the troops at Shanghai, until such time as the Government at Pekin should inflict on Li the punishment that was his due."

Gordon not only resigned his command, but refused with indignation a large sum of money, a medal of the highest class, and other rewards pressed upon him. When the Emperor's messengers entered his presence with the Imperial treasure, he drove them out with his "magic wand" or staff. To the flattering Imperial decrees he returned the following answer :—"Major Gordon receives the approbation of his Majesty the Emperor with every gratification, but regrets most sincerely that, owing to the circumstances which occurred since the capture of Soochow, he is unable to receive any mark of his Majesty the

D

Emperor's recognition, and, therefore, respectfully
begs his Majesty to receive his thanks for his intended
kindness, and to allow him to decline the same."
The conduct of Li in putting the Wangs to death has
been defended by the Imperialists on the ground that
they had become insolent and threatening, and that
it was dangerous to allow them to live; but there is
no doubt that Gordon was led to believe his views
with respect to their safety would be respected. In
any case, as one of his biographers has observed,
"nothing can be advanced in palliation of Li's beha-
viour in making use of Gordon as a negotiator between
himself and the men he had made up his mind to
massacre."

For two months Gordon remained inactive, and
during this time the Tai-pings were gradually recovering from the severe defeats inflicted on them. Then
Gordon reconsidered his position, and came to the
conclusion that in the cause of humanity he could no
longer remain quiescent. Explanations were likewise tendered him which somewhat modified the
severity of his attitude on the question of the slaughter
of the kings. But before resuming his command he
insisted that Li-Hung-Chang should issue a proclamation exonerating him from all participation in the
massacre. Writing to Sir Frederick Bruce, Gordon
stated that he had determined to act immediately,
and gave the following as the reasons which actuated
him :—" I know of a certainty that Burgevine medi-
tates a return to the rebels ; that there are upwards

of 300 Europeans ready to join them, of no character, and that the Futai (Governor Li) will not accept another British officer if I leave the service ; and therefore the Government may have some foreigner put in, or else the force put under men of Ward's and Burgevine's stamp, of whose action at times we should never feel certain."

Sir Frederick Bruce communicated with the Chinese Government, and obtained a promise from them that, when employing a foreign officer, they should strictly observe the rules of warfare as practised among foreign nations. This being done, he gave his support and approval to Gordon, who forthwith, at the earnest entreaties of Li, resumed the conduct of the campaign. He took the field on the 19th of February, 1864, at a time when the western half of the rebel country was still in the hands of the Tai-pings.

It is rather strange that during these later operations, when Gordon was less hampered by Chinese interference, the Ever-Victorious Army sustained more than one serious reverse in the field. This was partly owing, no doubt, to a lack of some of the resources he previously enjoyed, as well as to the difficulty of obtaining supplies on the march. Nanking was the ultimate object of the expedition, and in the outset Gordon secured victories at Yesing and Liyang. Then came the first defeat, at Kintang, a place held by the most desperate of the rebels. It was attacked by Gordon with a force greatly inferior to that of the rebels, and the Imperialists were repulsed with heavy loss. Gordon was severely wounded in the leg while leading the assaults. One of his men cried out that the Commander was wounded, but Gordon sternly ordered him to be silent, and went on giving orders until he nearly fainted from loss of blood. At last, Andrew Moffit, principal medical officer to the force, came out and carried him by main force into his boat; but even then Gordon struggled to get away. Major Brown and Major Kirkham were also severely wounded during the attack, while Major Taite and Captain Banning were killed. The Emperor issued a sympathetic proclamation, regretting Gordon's disablement and commanding him to rest.

But his rest was brief indeed. He was speedily on the warpath again, being the more eager for the fray when he ascertained that the Faithful King had occupied Fushou, the scene of his own first victory. Though still disabled by his wound, he pressed forward for Woosich, accompanied by his light artillery and a regiment only 400 strong, together with 600 Liyang men, who were formerly Tai-pings. After driving the rebels from a number of burning villages, where they had wrought terrible havoc, Gordon found himself at Waissoo. The rebels had resolved upon obtaining possession of Quinsan, and this was the centre of the movement. Gordon's officers, unfortunately, separated their forces, and when the Tai-pings came out of their ambush in thousands, the newly-

-aised Liyang regiment fled, together with the 4th, which was regarded as the best regiment of the Ever-Victorious Army. Great numbers were killed and taken prisoners, and when Gordon arrived at the enemy's position with his artillery, he found himself unsupported and in imminent danger.

Withdrawing some thirteen miles to the south-west, Gordon now ordered up his 3rd regiment, and having brought his demoralised troops into something like order, he once more encamped near Waissoo, where he was joined by Li-Hung-Chang with about 6000 Imperialists. Meanwhile, the Imperialist forces elsewhere had been rendering excellent service, though, unhappily, at the loss of General Ching, who was mortally wounded in storming Kashing-fu, greatly to the regret of Gordon, who shed tears on being informed of the fact. Though they frequently differed, there was a strong mutual attachment between them.

By a clever manœuvre Gordon severely defeated the rebels at Waissoo, this being an important point gained in crushing the rebellion. Chanchu-fu was the next point to be attacked, but on the night of the 25th of April, when Gordon and his artillery officer, Major Tapp, were superintending the construction of a battery, some of the Imperialists treacherously opened fire upon them. This fire was returned by the Tai-pings, so that the leader was between two opposing fires. "Many of the sappers were killed and wounded. Major Tapp received a ball in the

stomach and died in a few minutes. Gordon escaped
unhurt, and proved anew that his was a charmed life.
The loss of such a man as Major Tapp, at this pass,
was a calamity equal almost to the loss of a battle."
Li-Hung-Chang himself also made an assault on
Chanchu-fu, but was repulsed with great loss. A
combined attack was next made, but the Imperialists
were again obliged to retreat. Yet another attack
was made by Li, and this would have failed also but
for the support of a storming party led by Gordon,
which opened the way into the city. Four Wangs
were taken prisoners and beheaded, a fate which likewise befell Hu-Wang, the savage leader of the Tai-
pings, who fought desperately to the last. The
garrison was 20,000 strong, and the slaughter pro-
portionately great.

But Gordon's losses in the various engagements
were also very severe. In a letter to his mother
dated the 10th of May occurred this passage :—
" I think if I am spared I shall be home by Christmas.
The losses I have sustained in this campaign have
been no joke ; out of 100 officers I have had 48 killed
and wounded, and out of 3500 men nearly 1000 killed
and wounded ; but I have the satisfaction of knowing
that as far as mortal can see, six months will see the
end of this rebellion, while if I had continued inactive
it might have lingered on for six years. Do not think
I am ill-tempered, but I do not care one jot about my
promotion, or what people may say. I know I shall
leave China as poor as I entered it, but with the

knowledge that through my weak instrumentality upwards of eighty to one hundred thousand lives have been spared. I want no further satisfaction than this."

The re-taking of Chanchu-fu took place on the 11th of May, which was the anniversary of its capture by the Tai-pings in 1860. It was the decisive action of the campaign, and one in which the besiegers sustained little loss. The capture brought the operations of the Ever-Victorious Army to a close, and that force was formally disbanded a few weeks afterwards. The manner in which Gordon converted the peasants of Kingau into excellent soldiers has been justly termed remarkable. In the brief space of eighteen months, and at a cost of only £200,000, the young major of Engineers had achieved a feat of arms which placed him in the foremost rank of the soldiers of his day. The complete collapse of the rebellion quickly followed upon the capture of Chanchu-fu. Nanking was taken on the 19th of July, 1864, and the leader, Hung, escaped capture by having taken poison a few weeks before. His son fled under the protection of two of the kings, but all three were soon taken and executed. The remnant of the rebel forces gradually melted away, and the insurrection was finally extinguished in the Canton province in the following year.

The value of Gordon's services was fully recognised and acknowledged by the Chinese authorities, and his character was altogether of such a high and lofty stamp that Li became his warm friend and admirer to the last. Sir Frederick Bruce, in intimating to Earl Russell that Gordon well deserved Her Majesty's favour, said:—" Not only has he refused any pecuniary reward, but he has spent more than his pay in contributing to the comforts of the officers who served under him, and in assuaging the distress of the starving population whom he relieved from the yoke of their oppressors." The Emperor of China conferred upon him the title of Ti-Tu, the highest ever conferred on a subject, and one which gave him the highest rank in the army ; and he also gave him the Yellow Jacket and the Peacock's Feather, which are Chinese equivalents for the Garter and the Bath. Addresses were likewise presented to him in considerable numbers, but he would accept no substantial rewards, and he returned from China in 1864, as poor as when he entered it—being, probably, the only person who had failed to profit by his own brilliant deeds.

CHAPTER V.

LIFE AT GRAVESEND.

WHEN Gordon reached England towards the close of 1864, invitations poured in upon him from all quarters; but lionising was most distasteful to him. He discountenanced even a friend's narrative of the Chinese campaign, and it was only his own relatives who were privileged to hear from his lips the story of one of the most romantic campaigns of modern times. But if he avoided ovations, he could not avoid all marks of the public interest in his doings, nor prevent himself from being distinguished by the appellation of Chinese Gordon.

At Southampton the heroic soldier spent a few happy months with his family, and then, early in 1865, he received the appointment of Commanding Royal Engineer at Gravesend (with the rank of

59

Colonel), which he continued to hold until 1871. Gordon himself stated that the time passed at Gravesend was the most peaceful and happy of any portion of his life. His official work consisted in the supervision of the new forts on the north and south banks of the Thames, which were then in course of construction; and during his period of service, the old batteries at New Tavern and Tilbury likewise underwent an entire renovation. These labours, together with the maintenance of official correspondence and the general oversight of all the barracks and fortifications in the district, naturally absorbed a good deal of attention.

But the whole of the time which remained to him he spent in noble acts of philanthropy. He devoted himself to relieving the want and misery of the poor, visiting the sick, teaching, feeding and clothing the many waifs and strays among the destitute boys of the town, and providing employment for them on board ship. He presided over evening classes which he instituted for boys whom he had rescued from the gutter, and his house was school, hospital, and almshouse in turn. To be poor, sick, or unfortunate was to have a sure password to his heart. He was never satisfied till he could place his "boys" in the way of getting an honest living, or could obtain for them berths on board ship. A friend once asked him why there were so many pins stuck into the map of the world over his mantelpiece; he replied that they marked and followed the course of the boys on their

GORDON READING THE SCRIPTURES TO THE INMATES OF THE GRAVESEND WORKHOUSE INFIRMARY.

voyages—that they were moved from point to point as his youngsters advanced, and that he prayed for them as they went, day by day.

Many of his pupils or *protégés* were not merely rescued from dishonest practices, but through him more than one youth was spared the consequences of having yielded to a momentary temptation. One of these typical instances related to a boy who stole some money from the tradesman who employed him. His master was on the point of having him locked up, when the mother came in intense grief to Colonel Gordon to implore his help in her dilemma. He was moved by her entreaties, and induced the master not to publicly prosecute the culprit. Colonel Gordon then sent the boy to a school for twelve months, and afterwards procured him a berth at sea. The rescued youth grew up into a man of excellent character, thanks to his benefactor; and he was only one among many who had cause to exclaim whenever Gordon's name was mentioned, "God bless the Colonel!"

An interesting sketch of Gordon's life at Gravesend was written by Mr. W. E. Lilley, who was a clerk in the Royal Engineer Department during Gordon's command. Describing Colonel Gordon's personal appearance, the writer observed that there was in it "nothing particularly striking. He was rather under the average height, of slight proportions, and with little of the military bearing in his carriage, so that one would hardly have imagined that this kindly-looking, unassuming gentleman was already one of the most distinguished officers in Her Majesty's Service, one who had attracted the notice of his superiors by his courage and zeal in the Crimean War, and who had won lasting renown by subduing in China one of the

GENERAL GORDON.

greatest revolts the world has ever seen. This last exploit had gained for him the name by which he was from that time best known—viz., 'Chinese Gordon.'

"The great charm of his countenance was the clear blue eye, which seemed to possess a magic power over all who came within its influence. It read you through and through, it made it impossible for you to tell him anything but the truth, it invited your confidence, it kindled with compassion at every story of distress, and it sparkled with good humour at anything really funny or witty. From its glance you knew at once, that, at any risk, he would keep his promise, that you might trust him with anything and everything, and that he would stand by you if all other friends deserted you."

The Ragged School witnessed some of Gordon's most humanising work. The boys hung upon his lips, and he made their sufferings and sorrows his own. He followed them to their own homes when they had any, and received them at his own when they had not. "The only thing that angered him a little was when some Pharisee of the Pharisees would give an address to the scholars in which bitterness and condemnation played a more prominent part than love or tenderness."

"His benevolence embraced all," wrote one who saw much of him at this time, and who communicated to Mr. Hake the deeply interesting details we are about to quote. "Misery was quite sufficient claim for him, without going into the question of merit; and of course sometimes he was deceived. But very seldom, for he had an eye that saw through and through people; it seemed useless to try to hide anything from him. I have often wondered how much this wonderful power was due to natural astuteness,

or how much to his own clear singleness ot mind
and freedom from self, that the truth about everything seemed revealed to him. The workhouse and
the infirmary were his constant haunts, and of
pensioners he had a countless number all over the
neighbourhood. Many of the dying sent for him in
preference to the clergy, and ever ready was he to
visit them, no matter in what weather or at what
distance. But he would never take the chair at a
religious meeting, or be in any way prominent. He
was always willing to conduct services for the poor,
and address a sweeps' tea-meeting; but all public
speechifying, especially where complimentary speeches
were made in his honour, he *loathed.* All eating and
drinking he was indifferent to. Coming home with
us one afternoon late, we found his tea waiting for
him—a most unappetising stale loaf, and a teapot of
tea. I remarked upon the dryness of the bread, when
he took the whole loaf (a small one), crammed it into
the slop-basin, and poured all the tea upon it, saying
it would soon be ready for him to eat, and in half-an-
hour it would not matter what he had eaten. He
always had dry, humorous little speeches at command
that flavoured all his talk, and I remember the merry
twinkle with which he told us that many of the boys,
thinking that being invited to live with the Colonel
meant delicate fare and luxury, were unpleasantly
enlightened on that point when they found he sat
down with them to salt beef and just the necessary
food. He kindly gave us a key to his garden, think-

GORDON TEACHING THE RAGGED BOYS. [p. 63.

E

ing our children might like to walk there sometimes.
The first time my husband and I visited it, we
remarked what nice peas and vegetables of all kinds
there were, and the housekeeper coming out, we made
some such remark to her. She at once told us that
the Colonel never tasted them—that nearly all the
garden, a large one, was cultivated by different poor
people to whom he gave permission to plant what
they chose, and to take the proceeds. She added
that it often happened that presents of fine fruit and
flowers would be sent to the Colonel, and that he
would never so much as taste them, but take them or
send them at once to the workhouse or the hospital
for the sick. He always thanked the donors, but
never told them how their gifts had been appropriated.
We used to say he had no *self,* following in that his
Divine Master. He would never talk of himself and
his doings. Therefore his life never can and never
will be written. It was in these years that the first
book about him came out. He allowed the author to
come and stay at Fort House, and gave him every
facility towards bringing out his book—all the partic-
ulars about the Tai-ping Rebellion—even to lending
him his diary. Then, from something that was said,
he discovered that personal acts of his own (bravery,
possibly), were described, and he asked to see what
had been written. Then he tore out page after page
the parts about himself, to the poor author's chagrin,
who told him he had spoiled his book. I tried to get
at the bottom of this feeling of his, telling him he

might be justly proud of these things; but was answered that no man has a right to be proud of anything, inasmuch as he has no *native* good in him—he has received it all; and he maintained that there was deep cause for intense humiliation on the part of every one; that all wearing of medals, adorning the body, or any form of self-glorification, was quite

GORDON'S HOUSE AND GARDEN AT GRAVESEND.

From Photo]   [*by F. C. Gould.*

out of place.   Also, he said, he had no right to possess anything, having once given himself to God. What was he to keep back?   He knew no limit. He said to me, 'You who profess the same have no right to the gold chain you wear; it ought to be sold for the poor.'   But he acknowledged the difficulty of others regarding all earthly things in the light that he did : his purse was always empty from his constant liberality. He told me the silver tea-service that he kept (a present from Sir William Gordon) would be sufficient to pay for his burial without troubling his family. But though he would never speak of his own acts, he would talk freely of his thoughts, and long and intensely interesting · conversations have we had with him : his mystical turn of mind lent a great charm to his words, and we learned a great deal from him."

One more incident illustrative of Gordon's deep human sympathy may be cited. There was a specially handsome gold medal, presented to him by the Empress of China, which he highly prized. It suddenly disappeared, and it was not discovered until years afterwards that Gordon had erased the inscription from the medal, sold it for £10, and forwarded the sum anonymously to Canon Miller for the relief of the sufferers from the cotton famine at Manchester.

In addition to his Ragged School, Gordon took an interest in, and visited, the Sunday Schools of the district. He also sometimes spoke at the Sunday evening services, getting directly at the heart of the people by his appeals ; and when he left Gravesend, the poorest of the men and women among whom he laboured spontaneously put their mites together and presented him with a Bible. On one occasion, Gordon visited a poor, wretched woman, in an apparently dying condition. He lighted a fire, made some gruel for her, and fed her with his own hand. He afterwards appointed a nurse to look after her, and sent a doctor to her. Such examples of personal service on his part could readily be multiplied. He would pay up arrears of rent for struggling and deserving people, in order to save their homes ; and he would send sick children to the Sea-Bathing Infirmary at Margate. He visited much among the canal population, and if he overtook a poor person on the road whom he knew, he would carry her heavy bundle, or make any friend with him share the burden.

In religious matters Gordon was cosmopolitan ; that is, he sympathised with all who followed Christ, but he never formally joined any Church. He was partial to the English Presbyterian Church and the Church of England, but he could find the good in all, and was ready to help all to the best of his power. In the Moravian Missions he ever took a genuine interest.

Of course, being human, Gordon had his faults, and he never sought to disguise them from himself or his God. He was sometimes irritable, and at times also too impulsive ; but he was ever straightforward, and transparent as the day. He was humble, unselfish, industrious, and had a keen appreciation of humour. His faith in the Father of all men was as great as his love for His creatures, and both were dominant passions with him. He was a reverent student of the Scriptures, and no man in these latter days more justly earned the Saviour's commendation for unobtrusive and loving deeds : " Inasmuch as ye have done it unto the least of these My little ones, ye have done it unto Me."

CHAPTER VI.

GORDON'S FIRST SERVICES IN EGYPT.

IN 1871, Gordon was appointed British Commissioner to the European Commission on the Danube, and early in the following year he left Gravesend for Galatz, in Bulgaria. Here, in this obscure corner of the world, he remained for more than two years.

At the end of 1873, a great and important change came. Sir Samuel Baker had just resigned his command under the Khedive, and Colonel Gordon debated with himself as to whether he should offer his services to the Egyptian ruler. His motives for desiring to go to Egypt were thus explained in a letter to his sister:—" I believe if the Soudan was settled, the Khedive would prevent the slave trade; but he does not see his way to do so till he can move about the country. My ideas are to open it out by

getting the steamers on to the lakes, by which time
I should know the promoters of the slave trade, and
could ask the Khedive to seize them.   I have been
more or less acted on by sharks, who want to go with
me for money.   I have told them that, if it is in my
power to employ them, they must belong to the
A class—*i.e.*, those who come for the occupation and
interest it may give them, and who are content if they
are fairly reimbursed their expenses ; not the B class,
who go for the salary only, and who want to make a
good thing of it.

" My object is to show the Khedive and his people
that gold and silver idols are not worshipped by all
the world.   These are very powerful gods, but not so
powerful as our God ; so, if I refuse a large sum, you
—and I am responsible to you alone—will not be
angry at my doing so.   From whom does all the
money come?   From poor, miserable creatures, who
are ground down to produce it.   Of course, these
ideas are outrageous.   ' Pillage the Egyptians ' is still
the cry.

" I am quite prepared not to go, and should not
think it unkind of God if He prevents it, for He must
know what is best.   The twisting of men carries out
some particular object of God, and we should cheer-
fully agree now to what we will agree hereafter, when
we know all things."

After much reflection Gordon decided to tender his
services to the Khedive, and they were accepted.   He
was appointed first, Governor of the tribes on the

Upper Nile, but later he was invested with the higher title of Governor-General of the Soudan. The Khedive proposed to give him £10,000 a-year, but he declined to accept more than £2000, the amount he had been receiving from the British Government.

For nearly six years Gordon governed the vast region of the blacks with satisfaction to the Cairo administration (which was notoriously difficult to please), and with credit to himself. He did much to restore the finances, and he inaugurated the necessary measures for the ultimate abolition of domestic slavery and the slave trade. This end he ever kept before him. The power of the Khedive on the Nile he firmly established by the use of steamers, while he consolidated that power in Darfour by the overthrow of Zebehr's son Suleiman, and on the Abyssinian frontier by a treaty with King John. At the same time he gained an enduring reputation among the people for his justice and courage. He had that great merit in the eyes of an Eastern people of being always accessible; and he inspired his soldiers with something of his own inexhaustible ardour and confidence. His marches, such as those to Khartoum and Gondokoro, were surprising.

"Gordon has certainly done wonders since his stay in this country," wrote one of his staff from Lardo. "When he arrived, only ten months ago, he found 700 soldiers in Gondokoro, who did not dare to go a hundred yards from that place except when armed and in small bands, on account of the Barias who were

exasperated at the way Baker had treated them.
With these 700 men Gordon has garrisoned eight
stations, namely, at Sanbat, at Ratáchambe, Bohr,
Lardo, Rageef, Fatiko, Duffli, and Makrake, the
frontier of the Niam-Niam country. Baker's expedition cost the Egyptian Government £1,170,247, while
Gordon has already sent up sufficient money to Cairo
to pay for all the expenses of his expedition, including
not only the sums required for last year, but the
amount estimated for the actual one as well."

Gordon not only established a chain of posts
along the Nile, but he brought steamers from Egypt
in sections, put them together above the last rapid,
and with their aid successfully accomplished the
navigation of Lake Victoria and Nyanza. He thus
greatly extended the work already begun by Baker—
that of opening up the vast regions of the equatorial
Nile, and the lakes which recent explorers had discovered. His extraordinary energy and resolution
enabled him to overcome all difficulties of nature,
hostile man, and climate. His every movement was
watched by the natives as if it were something
miraculous, and he was styled " the little Khedive."

Of course he met with numerous adventures, and
suffered innumerable trials in carrying out his operations. Some of his best men were lost, and the
climate was trying to all. But having accomplished
most of his objects, that is as regards settling
stations, he was able to write home in April, 1876:
" I have definitely, I hope, settled the stations along

the line from Duffli to Lardo.   Lardo and Duffli are
termini.   Rageef, Badden, Moogie, and Tyoo (a new
station he had just made) are postal stations ; and
Zaboré and Kerri are main stations, and possess
passages across the river, and enable raids to be
made on the east bank, where a vast extent of
country exists.   Through this country used to pass
the old land road south."

His most valuable assistant, an Italian named
Gessi, sailed round the Victoria Nyanza in nine days,
and found it 140 miles long by 50 wide.   The natives
were hostile, and took Gessi for a fiend because of
his colour.   But at Unyoro the chiefs sent in their
submission, and all was peace.   Fired by what
Dr. Schweinfurth had written as to Lake Albert
Nyanza possibly belonging to the Nile basin, Gordon
went on an exploring expedition to the Lake in July.
He found Baker's maps wonderfully correct, but he
failed to discover a point of view which would command a general panoramic prospect of the Lake.
Early in October he visited Magungo, Murchison
Falls, and Chibero, in order to form a line of posts
from the Victoria Nile, or Somerset River, to the
Lake.   Then he returned to Khartoum, proceeding
from there by way of Esneh to Alexandria, and from
thence to England.

Perceiving that his efforts to suppress the slave
trade must remain unsuccessful unless his powers
were extended to the vast plain countries lying west
of the Nile basin—Kordofan and Darfour—Gordon

felt that his work was at present ended. When it became known after his arrival in London that he had not decided to resume his campaign in Upper Egypt, public opinion began to mark him out for the Governorship of Bulgaria.

But the gallant soldier would do nothing without first consulting the Khedive, although he was firm in his determination not to return to Central Africa without enlarged powers. He could not deal successfully with slavery so long as Ismail Pasha Yacoub remained Governor-General of the Soudan. However, he went out to Cairo in February, 1877, and matters were arranged to his entire satisfaction. Ismail was removed, and Gordon was appointed Governor-General of the Soudan, with Darfour and the provinces of the Equator—a district 1640 miles long and nearly 700 wide. He had in fact unlimited powers over a region which stretched from the second cataract of the Nile to the Great Lakes, and from the Red Sea to the head-waters of the streams that fell into Lake Tchad. "He was to have three deputies, one for the Soudan, one for Darfour, and one for the Red Sea littoral and Eastern Soudan; and it was formally declared that the objects of his governance were the improvement of the means of communication, and the absolute suppression of slavery. He was furthermore deputed to look into the Abyssinian affairs, and empowered to enter into negotiations with King John with a view to the settlement of matters in dispute between Abyssinia and Egypt."

In fulfilling his new and arduous duties, Gordon spent three years in traversing in all directions the

GORDON AND HIS CAMEL.

vast territory placed under his control.   We learn that now he was engaged in settling a frontier dispute

with the Abyssinian feudatories in the East ; and now
swooping down with scanty escorts upon some slave
raider or rebellious chieftain in Western Darfour.   He
appeared for months together to live on the back of
his camel.   " Neither the numbers of his enemies nor
the fiercest sun of terrible deserts could check his
energy.   His presence, multiplied by incessant toil
into twenty times the reality, awed the wild tribes into
obedience, and for the first time in its history the
Soudan seemed to feel that law and justice were
united with Government."   Gordon's letters to his
sister at this period were deeply interesting; the
following will show some of the difficulties he had to
contend with :—

"EN ROUTE TO SHAKA, 11*th September*, 1877.—
I had at Dara 2000 troops of only mediocre sort ; all
were timid, the fort bad, and I had not the least confidence of victory if it came to war.   I rode to
the slaves' camp with fifty men, and saw their troops.
I should estimate their number to be about 4000.
I told Zebehr's son and his chief to come to Dara;
they came, and I told them I knew they meant
to revolt, that I would break them up; but they
should be paid for their arms.   They left me, and
then wrote to give in.   Then came three days of
doubts and fears.   Half were for attacking me, the
other half for giving in.   The result is that, I think,
they have all given in, and I am on my way to Shaka,
their headquarters, with four camps.

"I thank God He has given me strength to avoid all

tricks ; to tell them (the slave-dealers) that I would no longer allow their goings on, and to speak to them truthfully.   There are some 6000 more slave-dealers in the interior who will obey me now they have heard their chiefs have given in.

"You may imagine what a difficulty there is in dealing with all these armed men.   I have separated them here and there, and in course of time will rid myself of the worst.   Would you shoot them all? Have they no rights?   Are they not to be considered? Had the planters no rights ?   Did not our Government once allow slave-trading ?   Do you know cargoes of slaves came into Bristol Harbour in the times of our fathers ?   I would have given £500 to have had the Anti-Slavery Society in Dara during the three days of doubt whether the slave-dealers would fight or not—on the one side a bad fort, a cowed garrison, and not one who did not tremble ; on the other, a strong determined set of men accustomed to war, good shots, with two field-pieces. Then I would have liked to hear what the Anti-Slavery Society would say.   I do not say this in brag, for God knows what my anxiety was, *not* for my life, for I died years ago to all ties in this world and to all its comforts, honours, or glories, but for my sheep in Darfour and elsewhere.   I confess to being somewhat tired of the length of the negotiations, etc., etc. ; but it is better to be tired and worn than that one poor black skin should have a bullet-hole in it.

"Let me add to this the fact that my black secretary,

whom I most implicitly trusted and so largely paid, had accepted bribes of upwards of £3000 in three months to influence me here and there. Needless to say, Nemesis fell on him."

Gordon, even in his busiest moments, thought deeply on religious problems. His letters are full of references to them. Here is one that may be taken almost at random, yet it is to a certain extent representative of all the rest :—

"13*th October*, 1878.—I wonder, if asked this question, how one would answer it : Would you like to go through life without a pain or trouble, and return to *perfect happiness* of a small dimension, or would you like to go through a sea of trials and return to *perfect happiness* of a larger dimension ? Notice, *perfect happiness*, whatever your choice may be. What would be one's choice ? I do not know ; man, and *hard* as I am, I would rather not answer the question, for really this life is a terrible ordeal. "

On his march through the Soudan to Khartoum, where he was installed, Gordon astonished the people by listening to all petitioners, and doing justice as he went. The news spread like wildfire, and he was besieged by suppliants of all kinds, and in great numbers. But he eventually arrived at his destination, and the ceremony of installation formally took place. The firman was read, the Cadi delivered an address, and a royal salute was fired. Gordon was expected to deliver an oration, but he simply said,

" With the help of God I will hold the balance level ; "
and this emphatic declaration gave great delight and
satisfaction to the people.

Mr. Hake thus describes Gordon's life at Khartoum :—" To his disgust he had to live in a palace as
large as, Marlborough House. Some two hundred
servants and orderlies were in attendance; they
added to his discomfort by obliging him to live
according to the niceties of an inflexible code of

WADY-HALFA.

etiquette. He was sternly forbidden to rise to receive
a guest, or to offer a chair ; if he rose, every one else
did the same ; he 'was guarded like an ingot of gold.'
This formality was detestable to him, but he made a
good deal of fun of it, and more than once, while
certain solemnities were proceeding, he would delight
the great chiefs, his visitors, by remarking in English
(of which they knew nothing) ' Now, old bird, it is
time for you to go.'

F

"His elevation had awakened a great deal of ill-feeling among the officials, and especially among the relatives of Ismail Yacoub. Indeed, it is told of the Ex-Governor's sister that on hearing of Gordon's appointment she expressed her opinion of the transaction by breaking some hundred and thirty of the palace windows, and by cutting all the divans to pieces. The second in command, too, Halid Pasha,

THE PALACE AT KHARTOUM.

was hostile from the first, and even tried to get the upper-hand. Need it be said that he failed miserably? He began with impudence and swagger, but he soon submitted and promised amendment. Ten days after he broke out again. His insubordination was telegraphed to Cairo, and he was instantly cashiered and sent about his business."

In one of his journeys between Khartoum and the marches of Abyssinia, a number of Gordon's camel-drivers were set upon and killed by the Barias, a wild tribe of the district.   Gordon himself escaped, but the dangers to life in these parts were such that he wrote home as follows :—" I have written to say that if any-thing happens to me, the Khedive is to be defended from all blame, and the accident is not to be put down to the suppression of slavery. I have to contend with many vested interests, with fanaticism, with the abolition of hundreds of Arnauts, Turks, etc., now acting as Bashi-Bazouks, with inefficient gover-nors, with wild independent tribes of Bedouins, and with a large semi-independent province lately under Zebehr, the Black Pasha, at Bahr-el-Gazelle."

Gordon was a man of extraordinary faith in God, and there is something soul-stirring about the way in which he set forth on his most perilous undertakings. " Praying for the people ahead of me whom I am about to visit," he writes on one occasion, "gives me much strength ; and it is wonderful *how something seems already to have passed between us* when I meet a chief (for whom I have prayed) for the first time. On this I base my hopes of a triumphant march to Fascher.   I have really no troops with me, but I have the Shekinah, and I do like trusting to Him and not to men.   Remember, unless He gave me the con-fidence and encouraged me to trust Him, I could not have it ; and so I consider that I have the earnest of success in this confidence."

When half way on the journey to Fascher, the Darfourians came flocking in to lay their troubles before him. He was quite alone, yet the natives already began to think that he wielded a power not belonging to ordinary men. He cheered them, and promised them redress. Then his Egyptian soldiers began to come in by bands and companies. They were only "nondescripts," but then there were no others. With about 500 men he marched from Dom-changa; at Toashia he thought to pick up 350 more, but he found them in a state of semi-starvation, and dis-banded them. The Governor-General went forward with the 500, passed unharmed through a hostile country where his force might have been cut to pieces, and safely arrived at Dara, where his appearance was hailed like that of the relievers of Lucknow. Here he had serious perils to encounter, for many of his soldiers were cowards, while others were plotting for his life. After making what arrangements he could for the safety of the place, he again set out, and at the end of a thirty miles' ride through bog and sand, entered Fascher with 150 men, to the great surprise of the beleaguered inhabitants.

With characteristic energy Gordon threw himself into the task of overthrowing the slave-dealing chiefs. One by one they were conquered, but the worst of all, Zebehr's son, Suleiman, still held out. Gordon's lieutenant, Gessi, attacked him again and again, and at length he was finally conquered. Besides Suleiman, there were other slave chiefs, Haroun, Rabi, etc., in revolt. The closing scene in the campaign is thus described by one of Gordon's biographers :—" Before leaving Fascher for Khartoum, Gordon had made arrangements with his lieutenant for the future government of the Bahr-el-Gazelle, presented him with £2000, and created him a Pasha, with the second-class Osmanlie. Leaving his chief to make his way to Khartoum, the new Pasha returned to his old quarters. Although the rebellion was not crushed even yet, Suleiman being still at liberty, the end was not long in coming. Early in July, Gessi learned from a deserter that the son of Zebehr was not far off, and was attempting a coalition with Haroun. Suleiman, the terrible Pasha at his heels, fled, with nearly 900 men towards the Gebel Marah, a difficult and little-known country; Rabi, with 700 men, retreating in another direction. Gessi had but 290 soldiers with him, but they were well armed, and flushed with victories. By an admirably forced march he overtook the enemy in the village of Gara. Surprising them in their sleep, and concealing his numbers, he persuaded them to capitulate. They laid down their arms in ignorance of his real strength, and great was Suleiman's mortification on learning to what a little force he had succumbed. By Gordon's orders the chiefs (including Suleiman and Abdulgassin) were afterwards shot. Rabi alone seems to have escaped. Gordon had made a hero of Gessi, and here was his reward.

" Thus fell the power of Zebehr in the person of his son Suleiman, and with it the whole fabric of his ambition. Gordon's prophecy was realised to the full.

Zebehr himself was tried in Cairo for rebellion against
the Viceroy, found guilty, and condemned to death.
But as the Governor-General had anticipated, 'nothing
was done to him.' He was suffered to live in Cairo,
with a pension of £100 a month from the Khedive.
This impolitic leniency did much to weaken the moral
force of these splendid and ruinous attacks on the
slave-trade of the Soudan."

During his march to Khartoum, Gordon had
learned at Fogia of Ismail's deposition, and received
orders to proclaim Tewfik Khedive throughout the
Soudan. He acknowledged the official intelligence
to Cherif Pasha, the new Khedive's minister, and
telegraphed the order to the several governments.

We next find Gordon proceeding to the Abyssinian
capital, on his mission of peace to the king. With
the greatest coolness and candour, the Governor-
General unburdened himself to the king in a way
that would have cost most envoys their lives. It was
something new to the sable monarch and his satellites
to see a man who absolutely knew no fear, and who
rebuked a sovereign for doing wrong just as he would
rebuke an ordinary person. One account relates this
passage of arms as having occurred between the king
and Gordon :—

"When Gordon Pasha was lately taken prisoner by
the Abyssinians, he completely checkmated King
John. The king received his prisoner sitting on his
throne, or whatever piece of furniture did duty for
that exalted seat, a chair being placed for the prisoner

considerably lower than the seat on which the king
sat.   The first thing the Pasha did was to seize this
chair, place it alongside that of his Majesty, and sit
down on it; the next to inform him that he met
him as an equal and would only treat him as such.
This somewhat disconcerted his sable Majesty, but on
recovering himself he said, 'Do you know, Gordon
Pasha, that I could kill you on the spot if I liked?'
'I am perfectly well aware of it, your Majesty,' said
the Pasha.   'Do so at once if it is your royal pleasure;
I am ready.'   This disconcerted the king still more,
and he exclaimed, 'What! ready to be killed?'
'Certainly,' replied the Pasha; 'I am always ready
to die, and so far from fearing your putting me to
death, you would confer a favour on me by so doing,
for you would be doing for me that which I am pre-
cluded by my religious scruples from doing for
myself—you would relieve me from all the troubles and
misfortunes which the future may have in store for
me.'   This completely staggered King John, who
gasped out in despair, 'Then my power has no terror
for you?'   'None whatever,' was the Pasha's laconic
reply.   His Majesty, it is needless to add, instantly
collapsed."

When he had concluded an agreement with King
John, Gordon returned to Egypt.   His resignation
to the new Khedive had already been sent in.   In a
letter which he received from Tewfik at Alexandria,
the latter expressed his great regret at losing Gordon's
services, but there was no love lost between them.   In

many respects, Gordon preferred Ismail, notwithstand·
ing his grave faults of government, and there was
considerable popular indignation against Tewfik.
The conduct of Nubar and Riaz, the Khedive's
ministers, also made it impossible for Gordon to
continue in his post. They complained of his
cessions to Abyssinia, and endeavoured to force
upon him a policy to which he was strongly opposed.

Accordingly, he surrendered finally and decisively
the office of Governor-General. When critics subsequently praised his beneficent rule in the Soudan,
he replied :—" I am neither a Napoleon nor a Colbert.
I do not profess to have been either a great ruler
or a great financier ; but I can say this—I have cut
off the slave-dealers in their strongholds, and I made
the people love me." But, unfortunately, after his
glorious rule ended, there was no one to carry forward
and perpetuate the work he had so well begun.
Although, when he left the Soudan, the public peace
was undisturbed, and the tranquillity of the Khedive's
latest possessions was apparently assured, it was not
long before the slave-dealers began to presume upon
his absence, and to resort to their old nefarious practices. Egyptian apathy and selfishness soon frittered
away the good results and the strong position which
Gordon had achieved by great and self-sacrificing
labours.

GOVERNMENT HOUSE, CALCUTTA.

CHAPTER VII.

INDIA, CAPE COLONY, PALESTINE, AND THE CONGO.

TO the astonishment of all those who knew the restless and soldierly instincts of Gordon, in May, 1880, he accepted the post of private secretary to Lord Ripon, who had just been appointed Viceroy of India. There was amazement in India, as well as in England, when the news of Gordon's acceptance of the private secretaryship became known. The official feeling with regard to the terrible enemy of all shams and charlatans was, that "with the arrival of Colonel Gordon, we shall have an end of favouritism, and all cliqueism will disappear from the face of official society." But it is easier to defeat a formidable army than to dislodge customs hoary with age.

The reasons which actuated Gordon in accepting the appointment, as well as those which led to his early resignation of it, are to a great extent shrouded in mystery. He stated in private, however, that the sole motive of his resignation was connected with Yakoob Khan. At the time of Lord Ripon's arrival in India, one of the chief political topics was whether Yakoob Khan, then a prisoner in honourable confinement at Murree, was guilty of connivance in the Cabul massacre or not. As the Viceroy's private secretary, Gordon examined the documents sent from Cabul in support of the charge against the Ameer, and declared that they failed to substantiate the accusation. Carrying out his reasoning to a logical conclusion, he held that if Yakoob Khan were not guilty, he should never have been deposed, and that he ought to be restored to his country. The authorities announced the impossibility of accepting this conclusion, and it appears that the officials of the Indian Foreign Office afterwards termed the documents sent from Cabul—"Worthless trash." This is understood to have been the reason for Gordon's sudden retirement from an uncongenial post, and on his return to England he made more than one attempt to procure what he considered justice for Yakoob Khan.

In one of his letters from India, Gordon wrote :— " Men at times, owing to the mysteries of Providence, form judgments which they afterwards repent of. This is my case in accepting the appointment Lord Ripon honoured me in offering me. I repented of my act as soon as I had accepted the appointment, and

1 deeply regret that I had not the moral courage to say so at that time. Nothing could have exceeded the kindness and consideration with which Lord Ripon has treated me. I have never met any one with whom I could have felt greater sympathy in the arduous task he has undertaken."

Writing to his sister, Gordon said :—"India is the most wretched of countries. The way Europeans live there, is absurd in its luxury; they seem so utterly effeminate, and not to have an idea beyond the rupee. I nearly burst with the trammels which are put on one. I declare I think we are not far off losing it. I should say it was the worst school for young people. Every one is always grumbling, which amuses me. The united salaries of four judges were £22,000 a-year. A. B. had been five years in India, and had received in that time £37,000! It cannot last. How truly glad I am to have broken with the whole lot; £100,000 a-year would not have kept me there."

In a letter written a little later we come upon this interesting autobiographic fragment :—"The more we see of life, the more one feels disposed to despise one's-self and human nature, and the more one feels the necessity of steering by the Pole Star in order to keep from shipwreck; in a word, live to God alone. If He smiles on you, neither the smile nor frown of man can affect you. Thank God, I feel myself, in a great measure, dead to the world and its honours, glories, and riches. Sometimes I feel this is selfish; well, it may be so, I claim no infallibility, but it helps me on my way. Keep your eye on the Pole Star, guide your barque of life by that, look not to see how others are steering, enough it is for you to be in the right way. We can never steer ourselves aright; then why do we try and direct others? I long for quiet and solitude again. I am a poor insect; my heart tells me that, and I am glad of it."

Gordon resigned his private secretaryship on the 4th of June, and two days later—by one of those singular coincidences which have rendered his life so notable—he received urgent telegrams from China, asking him to go there. His old colleague, Li-Hung-Chang, desired his presence, for war was imminent between Russia and China. Gordon safely arrived at Canton, and went on to Shanghai, Tientsin, and Hong-Kong. He is credited with having inspired the Chinese with peaceful views at a most fateful moment; and his presence in the Celestial Empire was also not without its effect at St. Petersburg. In view of the eventualities of war, he counselled the Chinese as to the kind of warfare they ought to wage, and they seem at a later period to have profited by his advice.

Gordon was back again in England in October, 1880, in response to a telegram from the military secretary at the Horse Guards, cancelling his leave, refusing to accept his resignation of his military commission, and requiring him to return to London. He was in South Wales in November, and on the 11th of that month, thus wrote to his sister from New

Milford, Pembroke :—"I was stationed here just before the war in the Crimea, and left this place to go out to Turkey.   I well remember, when ordered to the Crimea, my sincere hope was that I should be killed there.   It is odd to think what I have gone through since then, and that I still retain the wish for the other world.   In *Gold Dust* is this paragraph, 'May I pass through *this world unnoticed.*' Take a shilling out of my box and buy it, it has some nice things in it.   The prayer to Jesus, 'to be delivered from the desires,' etc., is very good.

"I have been down to the ferry behind the fort ; the old ferryman remembered my being there, for he said, 'Are you the gent who used to walk across the stream right through the water ? '   I said ' Yes.'

"Nearly every one I knew is dead.   Odd ! when I am living and have been through such dangers.   This confirms one's belief that, till God has no use for you, He will keep you here ; and if He does not want you here, He evidently will be pleased to have you in those other worlds I speak of.   When I get alone, I think much more of God and His directing power. One's capacity is infinite, as one's being is, and one cannot be filled but by infinity."

Towards the close of the year 1880, Gordon gave up a cherished idea of going to Syria, and instead visited Ireland, intent upon relieving some of the misery of that unhappy country.   He was so struck by the terrible scenes of poverty which he witnessed in the south and west of the island, that he propounded a scheme of land-law improvement. Although it met at the time with bitter ridicule or silence, it was afterwards largely made the basis of legislation ; but his views did not tend to make their holder acceptable in the eyes of the authorities, and to escape the necessity of accepting some insignificant routine appointment at home, Gordon volunteered to take another officer's duty in the Mauritius. For more than a year he remained in this island, unnoticed and unthought of, and fulfilling an exceedingly irksome task, but on his attaining the rank of Major-General he was relieved from his post.

Gordon was deeply moved on receiving the news of the death of Gessi Pasha, his faithful friend in the Soudan. Gessi died at Suez on the 30th of April, 1881, from an illness caused by his terrible privations on the Bahr Gazelle River, where 400 of his followers died from hunger. This loss meant a practical termination to all the good which Gordon had achieved in the Soudan, and which Gessi had striven to perpetuate.

In February, 1882, the Cape authorities having trouble upon their hands in Basutoland, applied to the Home Government to grant them the services of General Gordon. The latter was consulted, and agreed to place his services at the disposal of the Cape Government on the understanding that he was "to assist in terminating the war and in administering Basutoland." When he arrived at the Cape, however, the only post offered him was that of

Commandant-General of the Colonial Forces, an appointment which he had previously declined. But as the post was stated to be merely temporary, he took it up, looking forward to later employment as adviser and administrator. He proceeded on the 29th of May to King William's Town, where he drew up an able and exhaustive report on the Colonial Forces, showing how the Colony could save £7000 per annum, and yet maintain a strong army. He began the work of retrenchment himself, by taking only two-thirds of the salary offered him, saying that the Colony could not afford to pay more. Next, he went up country and reported on the trekking of the Boers into native territory, and on the condition of the native holdings in the Transkei. He likewise drew up a third memorandum to the effect that the natives were goaded into rebellion by the badness and inefficiency of the magistracy; but the remedies he suggested were not acted upon.

After great pressure, Gordon went to Basutoland in September, and visited the chief Masupha, with the object of arranging a pacification. He went unarmed, and it is a marvel how he returned alive, for the Cape authorities, while employing him as a peacemaker, were at the same time egging on other chiefs to attack Masupha. Mr. Hake remarks that " Gordon's power of inspiring savages with confidence in his complete uprightness probably saved his life at this desperate pass, as at so many others in so many lands. Masupha, seeing his guest to be no less mortified and astounded than himself, allowed him to depart as he had come." On his return journey, Gordon telegraphed to the Cape Premier that he was placed in a false position, and as he could do no good he must resign. The Premier accepted his resignation, stating that though the General's purposes were good, considering the circumstances under which they were made, they were not such as Government could adopt or Parliament sanction.

The failure of his mission was due to others, and these South African experiences seemed to have intensified Gordon's reserve and strengthened his resolve to live apart from his fellow-men. He had long yearned for rest, and now, after a very brief visit to England, he left for Palestine, where he resided principally at Jaffa during the whole of 1883. Nevertheless, he visited the chief places in the Holy Land which are of supreme interest to all Christians. He passed his time mostly in meditation on the meaning of the Book of Revelation, and also in considering the condition of the Turkish Empire. He took a keen interest in the Egyptian question, and "followed each move on the political chess-board at Cairo with great attention and intimate local knowledge."

Gordon returned suddenly to Europe in December, 1883, and it was not long before it became known that he had accepted a command from the King of the Belgians to proceed to the Congo. About three years before, King Leopold had conferred with Gordon concerning a scheme for the administration of certain territory on the Congo, and so perpetuating in these latitudes the memory of his dead son. Being now appealed to by the King to fulfil his promise, he put by his studies, postponed schemes which he had formed for the benefit of the London poor, and prepared, with the assent of the British Government, to set out for the Congo. The fulfilment of his promise was rendered all the more pleasing to him by the frank and generous manner in which the King met every wish and accepted all the responsibilities of General Gordon's transfer from the English army to his own, including the settlement of a sum of £7000 upon his heirs.

Gordon conceived and drew up for his own personal satisfaction a scheme for the suppression of the slave trade by means of armed levies raised on the Congo for the conquest or subjugation of the great slave-capturing people, the Niam-Niam. The details of this scheme, as given by himself, were published in the *Times ;* and although they were not destined to be realised, they were interesting as a project of warm-hearted philanthropy. In the question of the commercial prospects of the Congo route he took little or no interest. His general opinion of the district was expressed in this remarkable sentence : " These equatorial regions of Africa are all the same, they have only steam." It is strange that Gordon's heart was never thoroughly in this Congo work, for even on the morning of his final departure for Brussels, he expressed the hope that "there may be a respite, but

G

in any case, if I live, I go to the Congo for the King in October."

But his destiny was fixed in another sphere. Gordon left London for Brussels, on his way to the Congo, on the 16th of January, 1884, but he had not been twelve hours in the Belgian capital when he was recalled by the English Ministry. The cause or causes for this had been kept a profound secret. On the 18th he was in London, and held a prolonged interview with the members of the Cabinet. It was not until after this interview that his own relatives had an opportunity of seeing him, and of becoming acquainted with the fact that he had consented to undertake a mission to Khartoum.

BERBER.

CHAPTER VIII.

GORDON AGAIN IN THE SOUDAN.

ON the evening of the 18th of January, 1884, Gordon left London on his way to Khartoum. At Charing Cross Station a few friends assembled to bid him good-bye. They had hurried down at a moment's notice, for his departure was so sudden that much of his baggage had to be sent on after him. Among those who bade him farewell were the Duke of Cambridge, who had known him from boyhood; Lord Wolseley, who had been with him in the Crimea; Colonel Brocklehurst, and Mr. Robert Gordon, his nephew, and Lord Hartington's private secretary. The new Commissioner was accompanied by Colonel Stewart, whom he had chosen as his military secretary. What a solemn moment it would have seemed, had the hero's friends known that it was the last time they would ever look upon his face!

Since Gordon had left the Soudan, four years before, events in Egypt had marched rapidly and disastrously for the rulers at Cairo. The Moslem populations had risen in revolt, defeating the armies of Egypt and isolating her garrisons. Mahomet Achmet, the False Prophet, had acquired great influence throughout the whole of the Soudan. Born at Dongola about the year 1843, he was for a time in the Egyptian Civil Service, but disagreeing with the Governor he became a trader, and a leading slave-dealer. At the prophesied age of forty, he claimed to be the Mahdi, or the Mohammedan restorer of all things. Gradually, at the Mahdi's call—the Moslem equivalent for a revolutionary spirit—the Eastern Soudan stirred itself against Egyptian misrule. In 1883, the Mahdi seized El-Obeyd, the chief city of Kordofan, and made it his capital; and on the 5th of November of that year, the Egyptian army commanded by Hicks Pasha was annihilated.

It was under these circumstances that General Gordon accepted a commission from Mr. Gladstone's Government to go out and endeavour to pacify the Soudan. The Duke of Devonshire (Lord Hartington) was War Minister at this time, and, of course, was chiefly responsible for the British policy in Egypt and the Soudan. But when Gordon accepted his mission, he was given a free hand. The Khedive appointed him Governor-General of the Soudan, and wrote to him to the following effect on the 26th of January, 1884 :—" Excellency,—You are aware that the object of your arrival here, and of your mission to the Soudan, is to carry into execution the evacuation of those territories, and to withdraw our troops, civil officials, and such of the inhabitants, together with their belongings, as may wish to leave for Egypt.

GOVERNOR-GENERAL GORDON.

We trust that your Excellency will adopt the most effective measures for the accomplishment of your mission in this respect, and that, after completing the evacuation, you will take the necessary steps for establishing an organised government in the different provinces of the Soudan, for the maintenance of order, and the cessation of all disasters and incitement to revolt. We have full confidence in your tried abilities and tact, and are convinced that you will accomplish your mission according to our desire."

Misunderstandings subsequently arose as to the extent of Gordon's powers, and the various members of the English Government appear to have taken different views. Mr. Gladstone said : "It was our duty, whatever we might feel, to beware of interfering with Gordon's plans, and before we adopted any scheme that should bear the aspect of interference, to ask whether, *in his judgment*, there would or would not be such an interference." Sir Charles Dilke said : " He is better able to *form a judgment* than anybody. He will have, I make no doubt, every support he can need in the prosecution of his mission." On the other hand, the Foreign Secretary, Lord Granville, telegraphed to Gordon three months after his departure to the effect that, " undertaking military expeditions was beyond the scope of the commission he held, and at variance with the pacific policy which was the purpose of his mission to the Soudan."

But even the work of pacification might require serious fighting before it could be accomplished, and Gordon read his instructions from the Khedive to mean that he had authority to act as he thought fit when any emergency arose. The English Premier practically admitted this when he remarked in the House of Commons, on the 14th of February : "The

direct actions and direct functions in which General
Gordon is immediately connected with this Government, are, I think, pretty much absorbed in the greater
duties of the large mission he has undertaken, under
the immediate authority of the Egyptian Government,
with the full, moral, and political responsibility of the
British Government."

The Khedive himself, in addressing Baron Malortie,
after he had appointed Gordon Governor-General of
the Soudan, made the clearest possible statement as
to the nature of his mission.   On that occasion he
said : " I could not give a better proof of my intention
than by accepting Gordon as Governor-General, with
full powers to take whatever steps he may judge
best for obtaining the end my Government and Her
Majesty's Government have in view.   I could not do
more than delegate to Gordon my own power, and
made him irresponsible arbiter of the situation.   Whatever he does will be well done, whatever arrangements
he will make are accepted in advance, whatever combination he may decide upon will be binding for us ;
and in thus placing unlimited trust in the Pasha's
judgment I have only made one condition : *that he
should provide for the safety of the Europeans and the
Egyptian civilian element.*   He is now the supreme
master, and my best wishes accompany him on a
mission of such gravity and importance, for *my heart
aches at the thought of the thousands of loyal adherents
whom a false step may doom to destruction.*   I have no
doubt that Gordon Pasha will do his best to sacrifice

as few as possible ; and, should he succeed, with God's help, in accomplishing the evacuation of Khartoum, and the chief ports in the Eastern Soudan, he will be entitled to the everlasting gratitude of my people, v 10 at present tremble that help may come too late. To tell you that he will succeed is more than I or any mortal could prognosticate, for there are tremendous odds against him.   But let us hope for the best, and, as far as I and my Government are concerned, he shall find the most loyal and energetic support."

Volumes have been written as to why Gordon, with the promised support of Egypt and England, failed, not only to restore order to the Soudan, but even to extricate the beleaguered garrisons.   His biographer, Mr. Hake, affirms that it was because Gordon was constantly thwarted, and never supported.   In justification of this view, Mr. Hake advances the following propositions, in his Introduction to "Gordon's Journals" :—   '

"(1.) Gordon wished to visit the Mahdi if he thought fit, but Sir E. Baring (our representative in Egypt) gave him a positive order from Her Majesty's Government that he was on no account to do so. Of course, as I have already shown, Gordon, in his position as Governor-General, need not have accepted this as an order, but he was, as he always has been, most anxious to conform to the wishes or desires expressed by Her Majesty's Government, when those wishes affected only a point of judgment, and not a point of duty or a point of honour.

" (2.) Gordon proposed to go direct from Khartoum to the Bahr-el-Gazelle and Equatorial Provinces, but Her Majesty's Government refused to sanction his proceeding beyond Khartoum.

" (3.) Gordon desired 3000 Turkish troops, in British pay, to be sent to Suakin, but Her Majesty's Government, advised by Sir E. Baring, who disapproved of the measure, declined to send these troops.

" (4.) Gordon, being convinced that some government was essential for the safety of the Soudan, suggested the appointment of Zebehr as his successor, and gave the most cogent reasons why it was absolutely necessary for the accomplishment of his mission that the appointment should be made. He reiterated his request over and over again from February to December. Her Majesty's Government would not permit the Khedive to make this appointment.

" (5.) Gordon requested that, in the interests of England, Egypt, and the Soudan, he should be provided with a firman which recognised a moral control and suzerainty over the Soudan. This was peremptorily refused.

" (6.) Gordon asked for Indian Moslem troops to be sent to Wady Halfa. They were refused him.

" (7.) In March, Gordon desired 100 British troops to be sent to Assouan or to Wady Halfa. In making known this desire to Her Majesty's Government, Sir E. Baring said he would not risk sending so small a body, and the principal medical officer said the climate would exercise an injurious effect on the troops. These troops were not sent.

"(8.) Gordon, for the sake of everything and everybody concerned, showed that the Mahdi's power must be smashed. Her Majesty's Government declined to assist in, or even to countenance, the process.

"(9.) Gordon, in a series of eleven telegrams, explained his difficulties, and said that if Her Majesty's Government would not send British troops to Wady Halfa, an adjutant to inspect Dongola, and then open up the Berber-Suakin route by Indian Moslem troops, they would probably have to decide between Zebehr or the Mahdi; and he concluded these telegrams by saying he would do his best to carry out his instructions, *but felt convinced he would be caught in Khartoum.* Sir Evelyn Baring, in his reply to these telegrams, recommended Gordon *to reconsider the whole question carefully, and then to state in one telegram what he recommended!*

"(10.) Gordon telegraphed: '*The combination of Zebehr and myself is an absolute necessity for success. To do any good we must be together, and that without delay;*' and he supplemented this by another telegram, saying: '*Believe me, I am right, and do not delay.*' The combination was not permitted.

"(11.) Sir Evelyn Baring telegraphed to Lord Granville that General Gordon *had on several occasions* pressed for 200 British troops to be sent to Wady Halfa, but that he (Baring), did not think it desirable to comply with the request.

"(12.) Gordon desired a British diversion at Berber, but Sir Evelyn Baring replied that there was no intention to send an English force to Berber.

"(13.) Gordon, foiled on every point, telegraphed a graceful adieu to Her Majesty's Government. Then came the fall of Berber, upon which Sir Evelyn Baring at once telegraphed to Lord Granville that it *had now become of the utmost importance not only to open the road between Suakin and Berber, but ' to come to terms with the tribes between Berber and Khartoum ;'* and Lord Granville telegraphed to Sir E. Baring that *' General Gordon had several times suggested a movement on Wady Halfa, which might support him by threatening an advance on Dongola, and, under the present circumstances at Berber, this might be found advantageous.'*"

We return now to the thread of our narrative, and go back to the time of General Gordon's arrival in England before he left his native land upon his last mission. Before sailing from Southampton he granted an interview to the editor of the *Pall Mall Gazette*, in the course of which he freely expressed his views on the Soudan question—the difficulties and dangers of evacuation, the cause of the revolt, its chances of increase, and the means for its suppression. " He laid special stress on the fact that it would cost more to retain a hold on Egypt proper if the Eastern Soudan were abandoned to the Mahdi or the Turk, than to retain a hold upon the Soudan itself by the aid of material on the ground. That Darfour and

Kordofan must be abandoned, he readily admitted;
but, considering the influence a conquering Mohammedan power established close to the frontier would
exercise upon the destinies of Egypt, he held that
the provinces lying to the east of the West Nile, and
to the north of Sennaar, should be retained. He
pointed out that, if the whole of the Eastern Soudan
were surrendered to the Mahdi, the Arab tribes on
both sides of the Red Sea would take fire and rise;
and that the Turks, in self-defence, would have to
face a formidable danger, inasmuch as it was quite
possible that the whole Eastern question might be
reopened by the Mahdi. At the same time, he in no
way accepted the False Prophet as a religious leader,
but as a personification of popular discontent, engen-
dered by a renewal of government under Turkish
oppressors. The man, he said, was apparently a
mere puppet put forward by Zebehr's father-in-law,
the largest slave-owner in El-Obeyd, and had assumed
a religious title to give colour to his defence of the
popular rights. Returning to the subject of evacuation, Gordon put the pertinent question: 'What
is going to be done with the garrisons in Khartoum,
Darfour, Bahr-el-Gazelle, and Gondokoro, whose only
offence is their loyalty to their sovereign? As the
army could not go to their relief, there was no
remaining there with their lives; so that there were
but two courses left: either absolute surrender to the
Mahdi, or the defence, at all hazards, of Khartoum.
The latter, in Gordon's opinion, was the only one to

be followed. ' There is no difficulty about it,' he said. 'The Mahdi's forces will fall to pieces of themselves; but if, in a moment of panic, orders are issued for the abandonment of the whole of the Eastern Soudan, a blow will be struck against the security of Egypt and the peace of the East, which may have fatal consequences.'"

Gordon was of opinion that the Eastern Soudan might be saved if a firm grip were taken of the helm in Egypt, and the first and best step was to set up Nubar Pasha, and to let him have a free hand. But while plans and theories were being discussed, the Mahdi was increasing in power, and the problem was becoming increasingly difficult of solution.

During the voyage from Brindisi to Port Said, Gordon prepared a Report or Memorandum, dated the 22nd of January, 1884, in which, reviewing his instructions, he drew attention to some of the difficulties and complications which were likely to arise in carrying out the policy of Her Majesty's Government, and asked for their support and consideration in case of his being unable to fulfil their expectations with exactness. Colonel Stewart also, in his separate observations of the same date, pointed out that, in view of eventualities for which it would be impossible to provide, the wisest course was "to rely on the discretion of General Gordon and his knowledge of the country."

As Sir Henry W. Gordon, the General's brother, has pointed out, Gordon accepted the policy of leaving the Soudan. He held that to reconquer the country and restore it to the Egyptian Government without securities for a just and honest administration would be iniquitous ; and that, on the other hand, to secure that object would involve an expenditure of time and money which could not be afforded, and consequently he then came to the conclusion that the Soudan might properly be restored to independence, and left to itself. After his return to the Soudan, however, he did not remain long of that opinion. " His heart warmed at once to the people whom he had faithfully governed, and whose affections he found, or at all events believed, were constant to him." Indeed, his appointment excited real enthusiasm in Egypt, while many an Arab exclaimed, " The Mahdi's hordes will melt away like dew, and the Pretender will be left like a small man standing alone, until he is forced to flee back to his island of Abbas."

It was Gordon's original intention to proceed by way of Suakin and Berber direct to Khartoum ; but he changed his plans and went first to Cairo, where he was met on the 24th of January by Sir Evelyn Baring. He here received from the Khedive the firman appointing him Governor-General of the Soudan, without which he could have exercised no control over the Egyptian authorities employed in that province.

Gordon suggested to the Khedive that a Sultan of Darfour should be created as a check to the Mahdi's rule. This suggestion was acted upon before he left

Cairo; and Ameer Abdel Shakoor, the heir, was
summoned to the Ghizch palace, and given back the
province which had been wrested from his father, on
condition that freedom of commerce was maintained,
and the slave trade suppressed within his borders.
The new Sultan having agreed to this, he accompanied
Gordon to the Soudan.   They left Cairo on the 26th
of January, and went by rail as far as Assouan.   There,
Gordon embarked for Wady Halfa, from which point
he intended to cross the desert for Abu Hamed, and
thence to follow the Nile as far as Khartoum.

Matters assumed a serious aspect when on the 4th
of February, Baker Pasha, with 3500 Egyptians and
a number of English officers, was defeated with great
slaughter by Osman Digna, in an attempt to rescue
the garrisons of Tokar and Sincat.   England was
blamed for this, though General Baker was not in her
service, but in that of Egypt.   Great solicitude began
to be felt already for Gordon's own safety, and all
sorts of wild rumours were set afloat.   The Sincat
disaster was brought before the English Parliament,
and Government were attacked in both Houses "for
their vacillating and inconsistent policy in the
Soudan."   A resolution was carried against them in
the Lords, but in the Commons they defeated the
hostile motion of Sir Stafford Northcote.   "The
reason given by the Government for not sending
relief to the garrison at Sincat was, that such action
might endanger the safety of those others which
Gordon had gone out to rescue."   However, steps

were taken for the immediate relief of Tokar; but before they could be carried out, the greater portion of the garrison surrendered and went over to the rebels.

Still, it was necessary that Osman Digna should be encountered and subdued. Consequently, General Graham, with a force of 4000 men, attacked and defeated him with serious loss at Teb on the 29th of February. Osman rallied his forces again, notwithstanding, but at Tamari, on the 13th of March, General Graham, supported by Admiral Hewett, completely routed the enemy. These decisive victories were regarded as a death blow to the power of the Mahdi in the Eastern Soudan, though it was deemed advisable not to withdraw the British forces.

Meantime, where was Gordon? It seems that on the 8th of February he arrived at Abu Hamed. His brother says that, on finding the state of the country to be less disorganised than he had supposed, and impressed by the confusion which must ensue if all traces of the Khedive's Government were suddenly effaced, Gordon made the suggestion that a sort of suzerainty should be kept up, and that the chief officers of the Soudan should continue to be appointed by the Khedive. A complete and abrupt separation would thus be postponed, although the control to be retained would be more nominal than real. As time advanced, this idea in General Gordon's mind became stronger, and when he reached Berber he was more than ever convinced that it was impossible to carry out his mission with credit, unless he was able to secure to the provinces of the Soudan some kind of government, in the place of the one it was intended to withdraw.

While proceeding on his way to Khartoum, telegrams and messages continued to reach Gordon, warning him of his danger. But he remained perfectly calm and unmoved. In reply to a communication from a troublesome chief, he said: "Meet me at Khartoum. If you want peace, I am for peace; if you want war, I am ready!" And to the terror-stricken garrison at Khartoum he telegraphed: "You are men, not women. Be not afraid; I am coming." The following proclamation from Gordon, addressed to the people of Khartoum, preceded his arrival:—

"Know ye that I have come to extricate the Soudan from the difficulties and complications which have befallen it, to establish tranquillity and prevent the shedding of Moslem blood, to secure to the inhabitants their prosperity, children, and wives, and to put a stop to injustice and oppression, which have been the cause of this rebellion.

"I have therefore wiped off all arrears due from you to the end of 1883; I have reduced to one-half the taxes due for 1884, as well as of all taxes introduced by Raouf Pasha, and have put a stop to injustice in order that matters may progress, and that you may attend to your avocations and increase the prosperity of the country by the spread of agriculture and commerce. I also give you the right to keep the slaves

H

in your service without any interference from the Government or anybody else. You should live in peace; do not expose yourself to perdition; and avoid following the Devil's path. Warn the inhabitants, and reveal to them the good news, in order that they may walk in the path of righteousness, and turn away from the Evil One. Whoever wishes to see me, let him come and dread nothing."

When the terms of this proclamation became known in England, there was considerable disappointment at Gordon's attitude with regard to the slave trade. But it now appears that he was strongly of opinion that certain preliminary steps must be taken before England could hope to do away with slavery in the Soudan. Certainly, this proclamation did more than anything else towards enabling Gordon to secure Khartoum, for immediately it reached the town the whole aspect of affairs was changed, and the inhabitants were eager to welcome their deliverer.

On the 18th of February, General Gordon entered Khartoum. In his first address he said: "I come without soldiers, but with God on my side, to redress the evils of this land. I will not fight with any weapons but justice. There shall be no more Bashi-Bazouks." Rich and poor alike were invited to his levee, and to all who had complaints he gave a hearing. All the books of the late tyrannical governor were gathered together and burned outside the palace, as well as all the kourbashes, whips, and implements of torture. "He visited the hospital and the arsenal,

and passing to the jail, flung open its doors. The
condition of the prisoners was terrible.   Two hundred
men, women and children of all ages, were lying
about in chains ; some were innocent, some guilty;
but most of these last had served a term of punishment far in excess of the law's demands.   A rapid
inspection and a careful inquiry were followed by an
order to strike off all chains, and set the wretched
creatures free.   In several cases it appeared that there
was no record of any charge, and the gaolers could
not even say what they had been imprisoned for.
One woman had been lying there for fifteen years for
a crime committed in childhood.   Many were only
prisoners of war ; and others, immured for months,
had been merely charged, but neither convicted nor
even tried."

Gordon established boxes wherein the people could
deposit their petitions and complaints, and he caused
the proclamation of freedom to be posted on every wall.
Next, he freed two important gates and proclaimed
a free market, and issued notices that half the taxes
would be remitted and all arrears of taxation wiped
off.   An order was issued that all Soudanese were to
remain in Khartoum, but that the white troops—with
their families and such Europeans as desired to go—
were to proceed to Omdurman, on the other side of
the White Nile, thence to be sent down the river in
detachments.   A negro who had served under Marshal
Bazaine, and received the Legion of Honour for service in Mexico, was with general approval made com-

mandant of the troops in Khartoum.   A peaceful and
contented spirit spread over the people, and Mr. Frank
Power, the *Times'* correspondent, telegraphed home
that Gordon was working wonders in Khartoum.

But while much was thus achieved, Gordon *knew*
that after he left, Khartoum must still have a strong
native ruler, or the bulk of the people would flock
after the Mahdi.   Therefore, he wrote to the British
Government, pointing out the difficulties which sur-

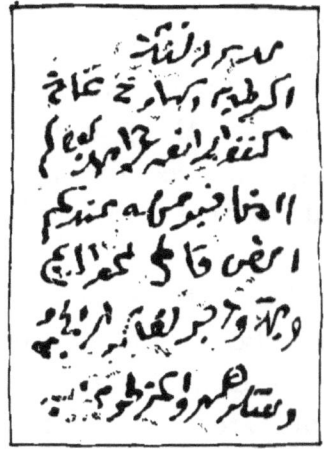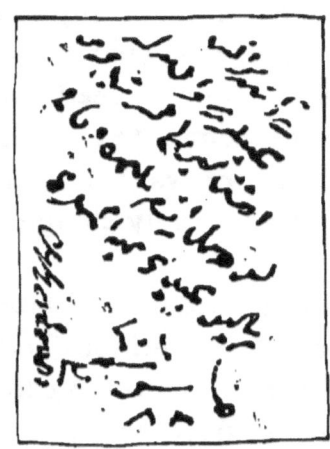

FAC-SIMILE OF A LETTER IN ARABIC FROM GORDON.*

rounded him—inasmuch as the garrisons and employés
were to be removed, when all form of government
would disappear—and urging in the strongest terms

* This letter, which is on thin Soudanese paper, the size of
our reproduction, was folded and placed in a quill, and hidden
in the hair of the messenger.   The following is the translation :—MUDIR OF DONGOLA,—Khartoum and Sennaar in perfect security.   Mohammed Ahmed carries this to give you
news, and on his reaching you give him all the news as to

he could employ that power should be placed in the hands of a single man, and that the man to be chosen should be Zebehr Pasha. Zebehr was Gordon's old enemy, and he was a noted slave-hunter, but he was a man of great ability and influence, and the only man who could hope to maintain a settled government. Gordon recommended that Zebehr should be made a K.C.M.G., and he showed how his ten years of exile, the influence of recent events, and his association with Europeans, must have affected and modified his character.

The Government rejected Gordon's advice, though it was backed up by Sir Evelyn Baring on the 9th of March as follows: " I believe that Zebehr Pasha may be made a bulwark against the approach of the Mahdi. Of course there is a certain risk that he will constitute a danger to Egypt, but this risk is, I think, a small one ; and it is in any case preferable to incur it, rather than to face the certain disadvantages of withdrawing without making any provision for the future government of the country, which would thus be sure to fall under the power of the Mahdi."

Meanwhile, fresh difficulties arose from risings in various districts, and the native chiefs would not come in, although repeatedly summoned to do so.

---

the direction and position of the relieving force and their number. As for Khartoum there are in it 8000 men, and the Nile is rapidly rising. On arrival of the bearer give him 100 reals Megidich from the State. — Sd., C. G. GORDON. 1301 (Shaban 28th). [22nd of June, 1884.]

Gordon again pressed the question of Zebehr, but the Government refused to sanction his appointment, fearing that he might join the Mahdi, that he would extend the slave trade, and that Gordon's own life would be in danger from his enemy. There were many who believed, like the General's brother, that Gordon's life would be jeopardised if Zebehr were sent up. On the other hand, a Cabinet Minister of high position was from the first in favour of sending him up, and so was Lord Wolseley. The Government, however, were firm, and they would neither accept evacuation with abandonment, nor evacuation with pre-arranged government ; they desired a third course.

While these questions were being discussed, serious events were transpiring in the Soudan. Gordon rescued the garrison of Halfiyeh—a small town some miles north of Khartoum—which was surrounded by 4000 of the enemy. But in the midst of great rejoicing over this, news arrived that the whole country around Shendy was in the hands of the rebels, and that Berber itself was threatened. Then, owing to treachery, a force which Gordon sent out to attack the rebels, was defeated with great loss. A rigid inquiry was instituted into the affair, and it was discovered that the leaders of the attack, named Said and Hassan, had deliberately betrayed the force to the rebels. They were tried by court-martial, and found guilty of communicating with the enemy and of having treacherously murdered their own men.

Large stores of rifles and ammunition were discovered in Hassan's house, and it was proved that both he and his colleague had stolen two months' pay belonging to the troops. It was necessary to make a severe example, and the murderous traitors were shot by the men whom they had betrayed.

Gordon's position all the time was full of danger. Khartoum was the arena of exciting incidents, and every day the palace was shelled or riddled with rifle bullets. Yet the General was untouched, though he frequently walked about on his verandah while the firing was going on. One day, three armed emissaries from the Mahdi arrived, with a demand that Gordon should become a Mussulman at once, and embrace the cause of the Mahdi. Of course, he declined ; but as it was now only too apparent that the policy of conciliation had failed, he immediately recalled to Khartoum all the Egyptian soldiers who were then on the way from Abu Hamed to Korosko.

Next, he earnestly pressed upon the Government to take some action, intimating that through their indecision many had joined the rebels, and that before long Khartoum must be invaded. By the beginning of April, however, he came to the conclusion that he could expect neither Zebehr nor troops, and that he would have to rely upon his own efforts and the faithful devotion of his followers.

THE FORT, KHARTOUM.

CHAPTER IX.

HEROIC DEFENCE OF KHARTOUM.

WHILE the British Government was in fruitless communication with Gordon, the power of the Mahdi was increasing, and he was recruiting his ranks both from the disaffected and those who would like to have remained loyal. There were not 500 men in Khartoum, nor indeed anywhere in the Soudan, who could be sent out against him, and the Governor had appealed in vain for 3000 Turkish Infantry and 1000 Cavalry wherewith to withstand him. Growing indignant, Gordon resolved to act alone, and to assume the sole responsibility. He was determined to hold by the people whom he had come to save, and to suppress the rebellion if possible.

The Mahdi advanced on Khartoum, whose inhabitants were already diminished by 3000 souls, whom

Gordon had sent away to Korosko.   On examination of his stores, the Governor came to the conclusion that he could stand a five months' siege, and began to lay his plans accordingly.   The soldiers received their arrears of pay, daily rations were served out to the poor, lines of defence were arranged, lines of torpedoes and percussion mines were laid, and as the Nile was rising, matters looked promising.   Several successful sorties were made against the rebels.   But four divisions of Bedouins, together with 500 soldiers, joined the rebels, and Khartoum was soon cut off from the rest of the world.   Money could no longer ensure the delivery of any message within the city.

For months now, all kinds of rumours were set afloat as to the condition of affairs in Khartoum, some asserting that Gordon and Stewart had been killed or taken prisoners.   But it has been since ascertained that early in August Gordon again begged that Zebehr might be sent to Khartoum, and Sir Henry Gordon used his endeavours to secure the attainment of that object.   Yet he was unsuccessful, although it was known that Gordon could not in honour leave until some form of future government could be decided upon.   That at any rate was the Governor's firm resolve.   To save Berber, two squadrons of cavalry were applied for from Suakin. The General's message was, "Send 200 troops to Berber, or you will lose it." A considerable time before this, Sir Evelyn Baring had said, "Under present circumstances, I think an effort should be made to help General Gordon from Suakin, if it is at all a possible operation." So that Sir Evelyn's views were in accord with those of the besieged Governor.

Colonel Stewart kept a complete journal of events which occurred at Khartoum from the 1st of March to the 9th of September, upon the night of which day he left, together with Mr. Power, the *Times'* correspondent. Gordon despatched Stewart to Berber, "in order to open communications with Dongola, and in order to carry on the necessary discussions in connection with the Soudan." Stewart and Power, with a party of some forty persons, went down the Nile in a steamboat, which was wrecked on the rocks of the Fifth Cataract. Going ashore they were murdered by the natives, plunder being the supposed object. The Englishmen fought bravely for their lives, but were overpowered by numbers. Stewart's journal was captured, and passed into the possession of the Mahdi.

The story of the later period of the defence of Khartoum is told in Gordon's own marvellous *Journal*—perhaps the finest record of the kind which exists in the English language. Here we get at the man himself, with all his moods, feelings, and aspirations. The *Journal* begins on the 10th of September, and ends on the 14th of December. It shows with the utmost clearness the position in which Gordon was placed, and reiterates over and over again that nothing would induce him to leave Khartoum until he had secured the safety of all those who had stood

KHARTOUM ON THE BLUE NILE.

by him. "I will end these egotistical remarks," he observes, "by saying that no persuasion will induce me to change my views; and that, as to force, it is out of the question, for I have the people with me, at any rate, of the towns which hold out; therefore, if Her Majesty's forces are not prepared to relieve the whole of the garrisons, the General should consider whether it is worth coming up. In his place, if not so prepared, I would not do so. I do not dictate; but I say, what every gentleman in Her Majesty's Army would agree to, that it would be mean to leave men, who (though they may not come up to our idea as heroes) have stuck to me, though a Christian dog in their eyes, through great difficulties, and thus force them to surrender to those who have not conquered them, and to do that at a bidding of a foreign power to save one's own skin. Why, the black sluts would stone me if they thought I meditated such action."

It is a strange picture which we now see, that of Gordon, alone, the only Englishman in the Equatorial citadel. Mr. Hake draws this graphic sketch of the Governor and his surroundings:—" Hunger and doubt were sore upon him and upon his people. But they still loved and believed in him, though, as he said, alluding to the long-delayed relief, 'we appeared even as liars to the people of Khartoum.' 'While you are eating and drinking, and resting on good beds,' he writes, 'we and those with us, both soldiers and servants, are watching by night and day, endeavouring to quell the movement of this false Mahdi.' The

old men and women had gone, and Gordon pulled
down the empty quarters of the town, and walked in
the rest.   Meanwhile, he had built himself a tower of
observation, from the top of which he could command
the whole country round.   At dawn he slept, by day
he went the rounds, looked to his defences, adminis-
tered justice, cheered the spirit of his people, did such
battle as he could with famine and discontent; and
every night he mounted to the top of his tower, and
there, alone with his duty and his God, a universal
sentinel, he kept watch over his ramparts, and prayed
for the help that never came.   Of his thoughts and
sufferings during these tremendous vigils, who now
shall tell?"

The apostasy of certain Europeans, who joined the
Mahdi and the Arab chiefs, drew from Gordon one of
his noble and characteristic declarations of faith.   "If
the Christian faith is a myth," he wrote, "then let
men throw it off, but it is mean and dishonourable to
do so merely to save one's life if one believes it is the
true faith.   What can be more strong than these
words, 'He who denies Me on earth, I will deny
in Heaven?' . . . Treachery never succeeds, and,
however matters may end, it is better to fall with
clean hands, than to be mixed up with dubious acts
and dubious men.   Maybe it is better for us to fall
with honour, than to gain the victory with dishonour,
and in this view the Ulemas of the town are agreed;
they will have nought to do with the proposals of
treachery."

A census taken at Khartoum, on the 10th of September, revealed that there were 34,000 persons in the place. Immediately after Stewart's death, alarming rumours—chiefly of French origin—were current in Europe with regard to the city and its Governor. One report announced that Khartoum had fallen, and that Gordon had exploded his mines, and blown himself and his army into the air. However, on the 14th of November, a messenger from Major Kitchener arrived at Dongola with a long letter from Gordon to Lord Wolseley, and cipher despatches for the Government. These were written on the 4th of November, thus showing that all was well on that date.

Returning to the story as told in Gordon's diary, we find him writing on tne 12th of September:— " When one thinks of the enormous loss of life which has taken place in the Soudan since 1880, and the general upset of all government, one cannot help feeling vicious against Sir Auckland Colvin, Sir Edward Malet, and Sir Charles Dilke, for it is on account of those three men, whose advice was taken by Her Majesty's Government, that all these sorrows are due. They went in for the bond-holders, and treated as chimerical any who thought differently from them." Two days later he writes : " The news of the near approach of the Mahdi has not troubled me, for if he fails he is lost, and there will be no necessity for an expedition to Kordofan ; if he succeeds, he may, by his presence, prevent any massacre. I have always felt we were doomed to come face to face ere the matter was ended.

"I toss up in my mind whether, if the place is taken, I shall, with God's help, maintain the faith, and if necessary suffer for it (which is most probable). The blowing up of the palace is the simplest, while the other means long and wearying suffering and humiliation of all sorts. I think I shall elect for the last, not from fear of death, but because the former has more or less the taint of suicide, as it can do no good to any one, and is, in a way, taking things out of God's hands."

It should be stated here that the English Government, convinced at last of the necessity for rescuing Gordon from his perilous position, despatched a relief expedition, under Lord Wolseley, in the month of August. His Lordship left England on the 30th, and as soon as possible after his arrival in Egypt he started with the expedition by the difficult and tedious journey up the Nile. The Government stated that the primary expedition up the valley of the Nile was to bring away General Gordon and Colonel Stewart from Khartoum ; and that when this object had been secured, no further offensive operations of any kind were to be undertaken. But Gordon ridiculed this view, holding that if the relief expedition was merely sent out to secure his own retreat, then the Government intended to abandon the garrisons. "I altogether decline the imputation," he says in his *Journal*, "that the projected expedition has come to *relieve me.* It has *come to save our national honour in extricating the garrisons, etc., from a position our action in Egypt has placed these garrisons. I was relief expedition No. 1. They are relief expedition No. 2.* As for myself, I could make good my retreat at any moment if I liked. Now realise what would happen if this *first relief expedition* was to bolt, and the steamers fell into the hands of the Mahdi; this *second relief expedition* (for the honour of England, engaged in extricating garrisons) would be somewhat hampered. We, the *first* and *second* expeditions, are equally engaged for the honour of England. This is fair logic. *I came up to extricate the garrisons and failed. Earle comes up to extricate garrisons and (I hope) succeeds. Earle does not come to extricate me.* The extrication of the garrisons was supposed to affect our 'national honour.' If Earle succeeds, the 'national honour' tnanks nim, and I hope rewards him, but it is altogether independent of me, who for failing incurs its blame. I am not the *rescued lamb*, and I will not be."

It was not General Earle who, as Gordon thought, was to be sent to nis relief, but General Wolseley. The instructions to the latter General, which ran as follows, leave no doubt as to the intentions of the Government:—" The position of the garrisons in Darfour, the Bahr-el-Gazelle, and Equatorial Provinces, renders it impossible that you should take any action which would facilitate their retreat without extending your operations far beyond the sphere

I

which Her Majesty's Government is prepared to sanction.

"As regards the Sennaar garrison, Her Majesty's Government is not prepared to sanction the dispatch of an expedition of British troops up the Blue Nile, in order to insure its retreat.

"From the last telegrams received from General Gordon, there is reason to hope that he has already taken steps to withdraw the Egyptian portion of the Sennaar garrison.

"You will use your best endeavours to insure the safe retreat of the Egyptian troops, which constitute the Khartoum garrison, and of such of the civil employés of Khartoum, together with their families, as may wish to return to Egypt.

"As regards the future government of the Soudan, and especially of Khartoum, Her Majesty's Government would be glad to see a government at Khartoum itself which, so far as all matters connected with the internal administration of the country are concerned, would be wholly independent of Egypt."

Feeling that the Government and himself held such opposite views as to the extrication of the garrisons, Gordon suggested as a solution of the problem that Tewfik Pasha should send up Abdel Kader Pasha, as Governor - General, to replace him. Lord Wolseley, acting for Her Majesty's Government, could then do what he thought fit with respect to the Soudan, its abandonment, etc., while he (Gordon) would be free of all official responsibility to the

people and to the troops, or with respect to money
affairs, etc.   This, of course, was not done, and
Gordon felt that it would be against his honour if
he were upon any consideration to leave the people
whom he had championed.   Gordon was strongly
of opinion that Englishmen made too much of the
importance of Egypt, and in this he was supported
by General Sir Lintorn Simmons.   "Egypt is useless
to us," wrote Gordon, "unless we have command of
the seas; and if we have command of the seas, Egypt
is ours; therefore, it is not worth bothering about.
We shall never be liked by its peoples; we do not go
the right way to be liked.   To my mind, if we looked
after the Cape and Mauritius, etc., it would be far
more beneficial and less expensive than wasting our
money on Egypt and the Soudan; but because
Egypt *used* to be important, we think it is always
so.   Whereas, the introduction of steam has quite
altered its importance, while the creation of other
naval powers in the Mediterranean renders that sea
no longer a question of the supremacy of France or
England."

Gordon's last scheme for the settlement and pacification of the Soudan is clearly explained in his
Journal.   Writing under date the 3rd of October, he
remarks :—" The more one thinks of it, the more impossible does it seem for Her Majesty's Government
to get out of this country without extricating garrisons
and establishing some government at Khartoum; once
having, as they have, come up to Dongola, they can-

not well go back from Dongola — they must come to Berber, and when once at Berber, as there is the river, they must come up here ; once here, they must go to Sennaar, or arrange to open this route.   It is of all things the most perplexing, and one does not see the end of it, unless we give the country to the Turks. With the best will and all favourable circumstances— *i.e.*, that it is found possible to abandon the country— it will take six to eight months, and with a terrible outlay, and one cannot think that even then it is a satisfactory termination if, after extricating the garrisons and contenting ourselves with that, we let the Mahdi come down and boast of driving us out.

"If we proclaim the abolition of slave-holding, we must proclaim it in Egypt as well, and then the revenue falls.   The Turks really seem the only way out of it, as a speedy way.   It would be cheaper to give them a million pounds than to keep our people up here, and there is no discredit to our arms if we take Berber and open the route to Sennaar, and then leave the country to the Turks, letting them deal with the Mahdi as they like.   I think even the gift of two millions to the Turks would be a cheap solution of it, and also a quick and an honourable one.

"As for Her Majesty's Government keeping the Soudan itself, it is out of the question, for you could not get men to serve here except under great salaries and supported with large forces ; and as for giving it back to Egypt in a couple of years, we would have another Mahdi ; therefore, our choice lies between

Zebehr and the Turks. Now, the time has gone by
when Zebehr, almost alone, would suffice ; he would
now need aid in men, while the Turks would need no
aid from us in men.   Therefore, give the country to
the Turks, when once you have come to Khartoum,
with one or two millions sterling (which *you* will
spend in three months' occupation up here if you
delay), make arrangements at once with the Porte
for its Soudan cession, let 6000 Turks land at Suakin
and march up to Berber, and thence to Khartoum.
You can then retire at once before the hot weather
comes on. Let 3000 Turks land at Massowah and go
to Kassala ; that saves you that journey. You would
be even saved waiting till the troops came from the
Equator and Bahr-el-Gazelle."

Early in October there was considerable excitement
in Khartoum, owing to the news that a Frenchman
had come up with two Arabs from Dongola to consult
with the Mahdi. Gordon thought it might be Renan,
author of the " Life of Jesus," who in his last publication
had taken leave of the world, and was said to have
gone into Africa, not to reappear again. There was
some ground for this, because Renan was originally a
Roman Catholic priest and a great Arabic scholar,
whilst he was also a very unhappy and restless man.
" If he comes to the lines," said Gordon, " and it is
Renan "—whom he had once known—" I shall go and
see him, for whatever one may think of his unbelief
in our Lord, he certainly dared to say what he thought,
and he has not changed his creed to save his life." It

was not Renan, however, but in all probability another restless and able Frenchman named Olivier Pain.

Anxious and worried by his position, Gordon wrote on the 5th of October :—" I should consider Her Majesty's Government were completely exonerated from all responsibility with respect to myself if they sent me the order, ' *Shift for yourself, we do not mean to extricate the garrisons.*' I should make my arrangements, and (telling the people how I am situated, with no hope of relief from them) should make a bolt to the Equator in six weeks' time. There would be no dishonour in that, for, as I had no relief coming, the very sequel of my staying with them would be to be a prisoner with them, and in fact my presence would only exasperate the Arabs instead of being any good. It may be argued, why not retreat on Berber ? I would rather not do that, for I would wish to show in a positive way that I had no part or lot in the abandoning of the garrisons, etc., and at any rate I should save the garrisons of the Equator and of the Bahr-el-Gazelle if I succeeded in getting away to them."

On the 9th of October there appears this item in Gordon's *Journal:*—" I feel sure that the Mahdi comes with the idea of negotiating ; if so, and one can have reasonable hopes of success as to the extrication of the garrisons, I shall negotiate, for up to the present time my original instructions are not abrogated, and I feel sure Her Majesty's Government will not wish any other campaign than is necessary in these parts for their honour ; but it must be remembered if, by negotiating, I get out the garrisons at the cost of the steamers, etc., etc., I must not be blamed, if in the future, by the cession of the steamers and warlike material, Egypt suffers.   Her Majesty's Government gave me clear orders—*i.e.*, 'Get out garrisons and evacuate.'   These orders have not been cancelled and are in force.   No official notice is given me of an advance of troops or of a change of policy ; therefore, I am justified in acting on my original instructions."

Next day, however, the Governor-General wrote that all information tended to show that the Mahdi's object was to starve him out.   "If the man would only drop his prophet's functions, we might come to terms; but he will never do that, I fear.   There is one good thing in the Mahdi's coming here—he will be easy of access if our Government wishes to communicate with him ; and also if he is defeated there is an end of him, without going to Kordofan.   I suppose our people at Debbeh must be aware of the whereabouts of the Mahdi at any rate.   It is an odd coincidence, the advance of the Mahdi and of the Expeditionary Force at the same time, and to the same place (Armageddon).   I have 240 men at Omdurman, and it is pretty strong.   It is not likely to be attacked ; for if the Mahdi won it, he would not have gained Khartoum, though it would be a trouble, as it would discourage the people."

Treachery having been discovered in Khartoum, Gordon made a number of important arrests on the 12th of October.   Next to his description of this stirring incident comes this curious little note, showing Gordon's tenderness for the animal creation. " A mouse has taken Stewart's place at table ; she (judging from her swelled-out appearance) comes up and eats out of my plate without fear. The turkey-cock has become so disagreeable that I had to put his head under his wing and sway him to and fro until he slept. The cavasses (attendants) thought he was dead, but he got up and immediately went at me. The putting the head under the wing acts with all birds."

On the 14th, Gordon wrote with almost prophetic insight :—" We are a wonderful people ; it was never our Government which made us a great nation ; our Government has been ever the drag on our wheels. It is, of course, on the cards that Khartoum is taken under the nose of the Expeditionary Force, which will be *just too late*. The Expeditionary Force will perhaps think it necessary to retake it ; but that will be of no use, and will cause loss of life uselessly on both sides. It had far better quietly return with its tail between its legs ; for once Khartoum is taken, it matters little if the Opposition say, 'You gave up Khartoum,' or 'You gave up Khartoum, Sennaar,' etc., etc. The sun will have set, people will not care much for the satellites. England was made by adventurers, not by its Government, and I believe it will only hold its place by adventurers. If. Khartoum falls, then go quietly back to Cairo, for you will only lose men and spend money uselessly in carrying on the campaign."

From a statement of troops, arms, provisions, etc., drawn up on the 19th of October, it appears that there were in Khartoum on that date a total of 8665 troops, including regular black troops, 2316; white, 1421; Cairo Bashi-Bazouks, 1906; Shaggyeh, 2330; and armed townspeople, 692. There were 12 guns, 11 steamers, 21,141 rounds of gun ammunition, 58 private boats, and 53 Government boats. There was a fair amount of grain and biscuit, and the money in specie amounted to £2900, and that in paper to £39,195. Reports of the near approach of the Mahdi were frequent, and it was said that Slatin Bey, who was with the Mahdi, was anxious to come in and see Gordon.

On the 26th, a number of officers and others arrived at Omdurman from the Arab camp. They stated that the Mahdi—who had been reported dead—was alive, and that there were with him Saleh Pasha, in chains, Hassein Pasha Khalifa, Elias Pasha, and all the Europeans. They heard a report that the British Expeditionary Force was two days' distant from Berber. Some days later, a report from Sennaar stated that the Mahdi had ordered all the Arabs to congregate at Khartoum from all parts.

The Mahdi was eight hours distant from Khartoum on the 4th of November, and this news was confirmed by the Mudir of Dongola, who had received a message from Gordon promoting him and his fellow notables a step in rank, and exhorting him to fight to the last, as he himself intended to do. From one of Gordon's messengers, the Mudir learned that the General had

illuminated Khartoum in honour of Lord Wolseley
and his men.   Further, it was reported that there was
plenty of food, and that thirty boats had come in
laden with grain from the Blue Nile, on the day of the
messenger's departure.   Gordon was very powerful, he
said, and was believed in by every man in the city.
Another messenger reported that the General was
very active in completing his measures of defence, and
that he was being joined by deserters from the
Mahdi's camp.

On the 5th of November, Gordon wrote as follows
to his sister :—"Your kind letter, 7th August, came
yesterday.   We have the Mahdi close to us, but the
Arabs are very quiet.

"Terrible news !   I hear the steamer I sent down
with Stewart, Power (British Consul), and Herbin
(French Consul) has been captured, and all are killed.
I cannot understand it—whether she was taken by
treachery, or struck a rock, is unaccountable, for she
was well armed and had a gun.   With her, if she is
lost, is the journal of events from the 3rd of January
1884 to the 10th of September 1884—a huge volume
illustrated, and full of interest.

" I have put my steamers at Metemmeh to wait for
the troops.   I decline to agree that the Expedition
comes for my relief ; it comes for the relief of the
garrisons, which I failed to accomplish.

" I expect Her Majesty's Government are in a
precious rage with me for holding out and forcing
their hand.

" King John wrote to me, but the Mahdi caught the letter. I sent you by Stewart a small packet with the bullet which came through my window, and I sent Brocklehurst also a lot of swords, etc., but all I expect are captured. All is for the best, and is overruled for good. I am very well, but very grey with the continual strain on my nerves. I have been putting the Sheikh-el-Islam and Cadi in prison ; they were suspected of writing to the Mahdi ; I let them out yesterday.

" I am very grieved for the relatives of Stewart, Power, and Herbin."

When Gordon penned the above letter, the relief force—unknown as yet of course to him—had just entered the Soudan at the Second Cataract. The greater portion of the Expedition was in boats built in England for the passage of the upper cataracts, many of which had never been navigated by any craft. Meanwhile, Gordon's activity, combined with the advance of the Expeditionary Force, roused the Mahdi to action. Feeling that he must strike a decisive blow at once if he meant to retain his hold upon the Soudan, he marched with 30,000 men from El-Obeyd to Omdurman, which was within a few miles of Khartoum, and called upon the Governor to surrender. Gordon's reply was characteristic: " If you are the real Mahdi, dry up the Nile, and come over, and I 'll surrender." According to some reports, this challenge was taken seriously, and the Mahdi bade his followers cross the Nile, which caused 3000 of them to be

drowned. Then began the attack of the enemy. It
was splendidly resisted by Gordon, with his twelve
steamers and 800 devoted followers. Desperate fighting went on for eight hours outside the walls, and
then by means of mines, which blew up the forts,
Gordon drove his foe out of Omdurman southward
to a place named El Margat. The Mahdi retired to
a cave, and prescribed sixty days' rest for his troops,
after which he prophesied that blood would flow like
water.

At this time Gordon, according to a letter of his
own to Lord Wolseley, had just provisions enough to
last him for forty days; and he had already dispatched
a number of his steamers down the Nile towards
Shendy, to await the arrival of the Expedition.

On the 1st of December, Gordon received a message
from the Khedive, from which he gathered that
Lord Wolseley and Sir Evelyn Baring were on the way
to Khartoum, and that they would settle the question
of the Soudan. To this he replied that it might be
convenient for the Khedive, but it did not meet the
case, unless the two British officials had a firman from
him, giving them authority. This they would never
have, for it would virtually make them Tewfik's sub-
ordinates. The best way out of the difficulty, Gordon
thought, was to make Major Kitchener, an excellent
man and an able soldier, Governor-General, subject to
the approval of the Khedive. Then England could
do all she wanted, and in a legal way. "But," he
remarked, "unless you have a superior firman to mine,

you cannot make Kitchener Governor-General (even if you had ten million troops), unless you declare yourselves the rulers of the land, which you will not do, because of the ninety millions' sterling of debt on Egypt. To my mind, this is the idea of *H.M. Government:—Expedition comes up to look after British subjects nominally*, but, *in reality, to settle future government of Soudan, under the pretence that Tewfik governs.* Tewfik telegraphs to me, 'that the British officials will settle future status of the Soudan with me *sub rosa.'* Now, of course, I may be wrong, but my idea is that the British officials will propose the *keeping of Sennaar, Khartoum, Berber, and Dongola, the non-interference with the Mahdi, cession of Kassala to King John, the leaving to their fate the Equator Provinces, etc.* And what the British officials propose, Tewfik will agree to: but then comes the question—as I consider the *proposal is unacceptable* (inasmuch as long as the Mahdi is alongside, no peace is possible)—I will not accept it, and will leave A or B or my and Tewfik's representative, to carry the proposition out ('*après moi le déluge'*). No one can blame me for this, for I should be a scoundrel if I accepted any proposition which would eventually give trouble to our country."

Firing went on furiously from the Arabs every day now. On the 2nd of December the Khartoum garrison replied with great effect, completely silencing the enemy, but Gordon nearly lost his eyes through a defect in his gun, which sent the fire into his face. The Governor's palace was a conspicuous object for

the guns of the Arabs, and they played upon it almost without cessation. Shells constantly fell into the town, but fortunately spent themselves without doing much harm. On the 3rd, Gordon wrote :—
" 5 P.M.—Artillery duel going on between our two guns and the Arab gun ; our practice is very bad. The shells the Arabs fire from their Krupp gun reach the palace garden, but the report of their gun is not to be heard. The Arab shells from Goba fall just about 200 yards short of the palace ; but in its line there is just the second of suspense (after seeing them fire), while one hears the soft sighing of their shells coming nearer and nearer till they strike. 7 P.M.— *Another battle* (the third to-day). The Arabs came down to the river and fired on the palace ; we could not stand *that*. 7.10 P.M.—Battle over ; we are as we were, minus some cartridges. 7.20 P.M.—Battle begun again, because the buglers played ' Salaam Effendina,'—the Arabs wasting ammunition. 8 P.M.— The Arabs are firing from the south at the Krupps on the palace ; they (*i.e.* the Arabs) are at least 4000 yards distant ; one hears the shells burst, but not the report of the gun ; they reached the river close to the palace."

Gordon thought of relieving Omdurman Fort, but had to abandon the idea. The enemy were far too strong, and were all round the Fort. On the 7th of December — which was the 270th day that Khartoum had been threatened or surrounded— between 300 and 400 Arabs were killed or wounded

in the day's engagements. "My belief is," wrote
Gordon, "that the Mahdi business will be the end of
slavery in the Soudan. The Arabs have invariably
put their slaves in the front and armed them; and
the slaves have seen that they were plucky, while
their master shirked; is it likely that those slaves
will ever yield obedience to these masters as hereto-
fore?" On the 18th he expressed his belief that if
Lord Palmerston were alive, or Mr. Forster was
Premier, neither would leave the Soudan without
proclaiming the emancipation of the slaves. On the
18th of December, 1862, Lincoln proclaimed the
abolition of slavery in the United States; and this
anniversary would, he maintained, be a good day to
issue such a proclamation in the Soudan.

Frequent reports continued to arrive of the advance
of the Expeditionary Force, but they were not to be
relied upon. Indeed, it is difficult to see how any one
could penetrate through the Mahdi's lines with such
information. Gordon was completely shut in, and on
the 10th of December he wrote: "We are only
short of the duration of the siege of Sebastopol, fifty-
seven days, and we have had *no respite*, like the
Russians had during the winter of 1854-55; and
neither Nicholas nor Alexander speculated on (well
we will not say what) but we will put it, 'counting the
months.' Of course it will be looked on as very absurd
to compare the two blockades, that of Sebastopol and
that of Khartoum; but if properly weighed, one was just
as good as the other; the Russians had money, we had

none ; they had skilled officers, we had none ; they had no civil population, we had forty thousand ; they had their route open and had news, we had neither."

From most points of view the defence of the besieged and solitary European was more remarkable than that of Sebastopol, with its legions of highly-trained troops. On the 13th of December, Gordon reluctantly came to the conclusion that if some effort were not made before ten days' time the town would fall. The delay was inexplicable ; and, as he said, if the Expeditionary Force had reached the river and met his steamers, one hundred men were all that he required, just to show themselves. The last entry in Gordon's remarkable *Journal* is as follows :—

"*December* 14*th.*—Arabs fired two shells at the palace this morning ; 546 ardebs dhoora! in store ; also 83,525 okes of biscuit. 10.30 P.M.—The steamers are down at Omdurman, engaging the Arabs, consequently I am on *tenterhooks!* 11.30 A.M.—Steamer returned ; the *Bordeen* was struck by a shell in her battery ; we had only one man wounded. We are going to send down the *Bordeen* to-morrow with this *Journal*. If I was in command of the two hundred men of the Expeditionary Force, which are all that are necessary for the movement, I should stop just below Halfiyeh, and attack the Arabs at that place before I came on here to Khartoum. I should then communicate with the North Fort, and act according to circumstances. Now *mark this*, if the Expeditionary Force, and I ask for no more than two hundred men, does not come in ten days, *the town may fall;* and I have done my best for the honour of our country. Good-bye."

There is something touching and yet dignified about these closing words. On the following day, Gordon drew up the heads of the arrangement he would recommend the Government to make with Zebehr Pasha for the future government of the Soudan. Then he despatched his *Journal* by one of his steamers, the *Bordeen*, down the Nile. On the same day that he made the last entry in his *Journal*, the 14th of December, Gordon wrote to his sister :—— " This may be the last letter you will receive from me, for we are on our last legs, owing to the delay of the Expedition. However, God rules all, and, as He will rule to His glory and our welfare, His will be done. I fear, owing to circumstances, that my affairs pecuniarily are not over bright. . . . *P.S.*—I am quite happy, thank God, and, like Lawrence, I have *tried* to do my duty."

We now turn to the progress of the Relief Force. For a long time its movements failed to justify the sanguine expectations of those in England. Conflicting reports as to its probable arrival at Khartoum were sent home. One report said it would arrive before the walls of the besieged city on the 14th of January, another fixed the middle of February as the time, while a third postponed the date as far as the middle of March. Lord Wolseley, convinced that matters must be hastened, offered £100 to the

K

regiment covering the distance from Sarras to Debbeh most expeditiously and with least damage to the boats. By the end of December a strong force had collected at Korti. Sir H. Stewart was despatched on his celebrated march through the desert to Metemmeh.

On the 17th of January, Sir Herbert Stewart, on his way to the Abu Klea Wells, defeated a strong force of 10,000 Arabs, collected from Berber, Metemmeh, and Omdurman. Unfortunately, our losses were 65 non-commissioned officers and men killed, and 85 wounded, as well as nine officers killed, among whom was Colonel Burnaby. After his brilliant victory, Stewart pushed on, and at Gubat, on the 19th, he encountered a still stronger force of the enemy, who were here some 18,000 strong. A desperate battle ensued, and the Arabs were ultimately defeated with great slaughter ; but Stewart himself was mortally wounded, and Mr. Cameron of the *Standard*, and Mr. Herbert of the *Morning Post*, were killed.

Sir Charles Wilson, who now succeeded to the command of the desert column, made a reconnaissance upon Metemmeh, but finding the place too strong for attack, he embarked with three officers and twenty men on the 24th of January in two of Gordon's steamers which had come down the Nile. The men on the steamers brought this message from Gordon : " All right at Khartoum. Can hold out for years." In explanation of this singular message, which was dated the 29th of December, when Gordon was

rapidly nearing the end of his provisions, Mr. Hake
states that it was written for the enemy, and that its

SIR H. STEWART'S CONFLICT AT ABU KLEA.

true meaning was that Gordon had come to his last
biscuit. The world did not know this, but the

Governor's friends were most apprehensive of his safety.

A messenger from Khartoum brought to the Commander-in-Chief a confidential despatch from Gordon, dated the 14th of December, to the following effect :—

" We are besieged on three sides, Omdurman, Halfiyeh, and Hoggi Ali. Fighting goes on day and night. Enemy cannot take us except by starving us out. Do not scatter your troops. Enemy are numerous. Bring plenty of troops if you can. We still hold Omdurman on the left bank and the Fort on the right bank.

" The Mahdi's people have thrown up earthworks within rifle-shot of Omdurman. The Mahdi lives out of gun shot.

" About four weeks ago the Mahdi's people attacked Omdurman, and disabled one steamer. We disabled one of the Mahdi's guns.

" Three days after, fighting was renewed on the south, and rebels were again driven back.

" Saleb Bay and Slatin Bey are chained in Mahdi's camp.

" Our troops in Khartoum are suffering from lack of provisions. Food we still have is little ; some grain and biscuit.

" We want you to come quickly. You should come by Metemmeh or Berber. Make by these two roads. Do not leave Berber in your rear. Keep enemy in your front, and when you have taken Berber send me word from Berber.

"Do this without letting rumours of your approach spread abroad.

"In Khartoum there are no butter or dates, and little meat. All food is very dear."

Wilson made a desperate effort to reach Khartoum in time, but was just two days too late. On the 28th of January, he and his companions drew near the city, but they were received by a tremendous fire, and the Mahdi's flag on the citadel showed that the place had fallen. Nothing could be heard decisively about Gordon, and Wilson was compelled to return. Lieut. Stuart-Wortley, in reporting these untoward events to Lord Wolseley, wrote :—"We could not land under such opposition, so turned round and ran down stream. No flags flying from Government House in Khartoum, and the house appeared wrecked. Only one man killed and five wounded in steamers. On the 31st of January, the steamer on which were Sir C. Wilson and all his party was wrecked about four miles above enemy's position below bottom of Shabluka Cataract. The other steamer had been previously wrecked on the 29th of January. We reached Gubat in small boats at 2 P.M., the same day. Fall of Khartoum on the 26th of January, he reports to be without doubt; but fate of Gordon uncertain, as reports are conflicting, but general opinion is he is killed, but no preponderance of evidence either way. Some say he is shut up in church at Khartoum with some Greeks. Fall of Khartoum has determined Shukriyeh tribes to join the Mahdi, so east bank of

Nile as well as left bank is hostile to us. The fear of
the English is great among the natives. General Earle's
advance awaited with anxiety by them. Natives say
Mahdi was very hard pressed for supplies at Omdurman. It is said by natives that he will have great
difficulty in persuading his Emirs to attack us.
Messenger from the Mahdi reached Sir C. Wilson
when in steamer on the 29th of January, telling him
Gordon had adopted Mahdi uniform, and calling upon
us to surrender; that he would not write again, but if
we did not become Mohammedans he would wipe us
off the face of the earth. It is said that Faragh
Pasha treacherously made terms with Mahdi, and
opened the gates of the city to Mahdi's troops."

The rescue of Sir Charles Wilson from the rocks
on which his vessel was struck was gallantly accomplished by Lord Charles Beresford. It was said by
some that if Wilson had hastened his movements,
and advanced more quickly from Metemmeh, he
might have reached Khartoum on the evening of the
25th. Sir H. W. Gordon, however—Gordon's own
brother—has completely absolved him from blame in
this matter, and shown that he did all that it was
possible to do under the circumstances.

With regard to the second branch of the Relief
Force—that under the command of General Earle—it
broke off from the main force to open the way to
Berber. On the 9th of February, 1885, it reached
Dulka Island, about 70 miles from Merawi. Next
morning it proceeded to attack the enemy's position.

The Black Watch, commanded by Earle himself, advanced over broken and difficult ground, and drove the enemy before them ; but just at the moment of victory, the General fell, on the summit of the ridge, at the head of his men.

The rest of the story as touching the Relief Force is soon told.   When Lord Wolseley had definitely ascertained that Khartoum had fallen, he telegraphed home for instructions.   At first it was determined that Khartoum must be retaken at all costs ; but other counsels prevailed in the end, and the General received orders to retire upon Korti.   The force formerly commanded by General Earle also now retired under the command of Colonel Brackenbury ; and towards the end of May all the English forces were withdrawn within the Frontier of Upper Egypt.

Slatin Pasha, in his thrilling narrative, *Fire and Sword in the Soudan*—published in February, 1896—amplified and corrected previous accounts of the fall of Khartoum and the death of Gordon.   He did not conceal his strong opinion that if the British troops had appeared three days earlier, their mere appearance would have sufficed to save Gordon and Khartoum.

So much for the Expeditionary Force ; but we have still to describe the closing scene in the life of the distinguished hero it went out to succour.

A FEW OF THE MAHDI'S SOLDIERS.

CHAPTER X.

THE FINAL TRAGEDY.

THE marvellous defence of Khartoum for nearly twelve months, was—as was well observed at the time—in every way worthy of the man who was not only successful in almost everything he undertook, but who made the simplest tasks appear honourable by the noble manner in which he carried them out. But the end came at last; treachery triumphed, and the hero perished.

It was to be expected, perhaps, that the most conflicting stories would be set afloat concerning Khartoum and its brave defender. One report said that he was killed fighting to the last, another that he was still alive, surrounded by a few faithful Soudanese. Then details were given of a desperate struggle and a general massacre, and these again were suc-

ceeded by a report made by a follower of the Mahdi
to Sir Charles Wilson, that Gordon was in his master's
hands and had assumed his master's uniform.   Dates
and incidents were hopelessly intermingled, but from
the general confusion one fact at least stood clearly
forth—Khartoum had fallen through the treachery
of Faragh Pasha, commander of the Soudanese troops.

Gordon was a great reader of character, and had
always mistrusted Faragh ; yet he had spared him
when condemned to death for treason, and, as he
never did things by halves, even in forgiving his
enemies, he took the traitor into his confidence again.
There is now no doubt that his confidence was
abused, and that Faragh made terms with the Mahdi,
and received the promise of a price for Khartoum.
On the 13th of February, 1885, General Brackenbury
received a despatch conveying the news that Gordon
was certainly dead.   The Mudir of Dongola was
also compelled against his will to believe in the fall
of Khartoum.   A native of Wady Halfa brought a
detailed account of the catastrophe to the leader of
the Relief Force.   He stated that Faragh Pasha, who
was before suspected of treacherously communicating
with the Mahdi, had opened the gates in the south
wall to the Niami men belonging to the great slave
tribe, who were besieging that side.

Many of the details given as to the manner of
Gordon's death were incorrect ; but a despatch dated
the 12th of February, and forwarded by a correspondent at Abu Kru, gave a fuller and more accurate

account of the melancholy circumstances attending
the fall of Khartoum, and the death of Gordon.
This despatch, which was all too soon confirmed by
Lord Wolseley himself, ran as follows :—" General
Gordon's trusted messenger, George, a well-known
Khartoum Greek merchant, who for months past has
been entrusted with all letters passing from or to the
besieged, and who has been living on board one of
the steamers sent here, states that nearly all the
natives' stories agree that General Gordon—on
hearing that he was betrayed—made a rush for the
magazine in the Catholic mission. Finding that the
enemy were actually in possession of that building by
the treachery of Faragh, General Gordon returned
to Government House, and was killed while trying to
re-enter it. Some say that he was shot, others that
he was stabbed. The Mahdi's people were admitted
to Khartoum at ten o'clock on the night of the 26th of
January. George adds that the rebels massacred all the
white people, men, women, and children, throwing the
bodies into the Nile, many of which corpses he and
others saw while with Sir Charles Wilson's party.
The families of all the men on board General
Gordon's steamers were also murdered. General
Gordon clearly anticipated his fate, for he wrote a
number of farewell letters during the month of
January. These were sent off in a mail-bag on board
the steamer, and given to George, who handed them
over to Sir Charles Wilson on the 21st of January.
Among the letters were one for his sister, and others for

his brother, for Captain Brocklehurst, Lord Wolseley, and Sir Charles Wilson. There were also six complete monthly diaries of the siege of Khartoum, narrating all the events that had taken place since Colonel Stewart had left him. In his letter to Sir Charles Wilson, General Gordon wrote that he hoped, by God's will, the English would arrive in time to save him and others, but feared they would be too late ; that he knew he **was** being betrayed, but was powerless to prevent it. His information was that Khartoum was to be surrendered on the 19th of January to the Mahdi. He could get away if he wished to run ; but refused to go, and would remain to the last. As he would not permit himself to be taken prisoner, there was nothing left but death. Khasen-el-Nous, the commandant with the steamers here, who has proved so loyal throughout, states that even had the English got to Khartoum a month earlier, they would have been too late to save Gordon, for the two traitors had committed themselves, and would never have awaited our arrival, as they feared that General Gordon would punish them. The people of Khartoum had despaired of ever seeing English soldiers, and tried to make the best terms they could. After the battle of Abu Klea, the Mahdi, no doubt, promised much."

Really authentic accounts of the death of Gordon now agree that he was slain at the top of the outer steps of the Governor's palace, either as he was going forth from the palace or endeavouring to re-enter it. Slatin Pasha—who is perhaps the only person living capable of giving conclusive and trustworthy evidence touching Gordon's death — corroborates this. He thinks that Gordon may have been taken by surprise at the attack made before daybreak on the 26th of January, 1885, but it is clear that he was killed on the steps of the Governor's palace. The hero's head, borne by three black soldiers, who were followed by a weeping crowd, was afterwards carried in triumph to Slatin.

The terrible events at Khartoum, when they became known in England, sent a thrill of horror and indignation throughout the country, and the Government was severely condemned in many quarters for its procrastination. Mr. Gladstone, however, who was strongly moved by Gordon's death, rose to the situation, and announced that it was necessary to overthrow the Mahdi at Khartoum, to renew operations against Osman Digna, and to construct a railway from Suakin to Berber, with a view to a campaign in the autumn. A Royal proclamation was issued calling out the Reserves. Sir Stafford Northcote initiated a debate on the Soudan question with a motion affirming that the risks and sacrifices which the Government appeared to be ready to encounter, could only be justified by a distinct recognition of our responsibility for Egypt, and those portions of the Soudan which are necessary to its security. Mr. John Morley introduced an amendment to the motion, waiving any judgment on the policy of the Ministry, but expressing regret at its decision to continue the conflict with the Mahdi. Mr. Gladstone skilfully dealt with both motion and amendment. In the Lords, a motion was carried against the Government, but in the Commons, the Government obtained a majority of 14, the votes being 302 to 288 ; yet many of those who supported the Government had previously voted for Mr. Morley's amendment, which was rejected. At a later stage, the Premier stated that no further operations would be undertaken either on the Nile or near Suakin, and that General Graham's campaign was to be abandoned, as well as the construction of the new railway.

Gordon was dead, and little good was to be obtained by endeavouring to avenge his death, as though that would wipe out our great loss, or remedy the evils of procrastination into which we had been led. Mr. Gladstone was almost universally blamed for the delay, but a calmer judgment will show that the chief responsibility for the blame should be laid elsewhere. There is no doubt that the information upon which the English War Office and the Foreign Office had to act was of a most conflicting character, and any Government—whether Conservative or Liberal— might easily have mis-read it. This fact should be remembered by those who condemn severely, and without thought, honourable men like Mr. Gladstone, Lord Granville, and the Duke of Devonshire, who would have been only too eager to save Gordon, had they known of his imminent peril.

The death of Gordon called forth universal lamentations. He was the great hero of the age, loved and admired by all. The leading men of every nation of civilised Europe mourned for him as tney would for one of their own illustrious compatriots. He belonged not to the English race alone, but to all humanity. There are few names in history with which so many striking achievements are associated ; and as he was but fifty-two years of age when he died, in all probability there was still a long period of noble service before him. It is known that the King of the Belgians intended to make him King of the Congo, and to give his genius full play in the task of laying the foundations of civilisation in that vast region. No one else could have done such work as this, for no other European ever possessed such magical influence over the natives of Africa. But all such speculations are now fruitless. The hero is dead, and we know that he had no fear of the last enemy of mankind. He could meet death heroically, and in the spirit which prompted these words—some of the last which he penned to his sister :—" Any one whom God gives to be much in union with Him cannot even suffer a pang at death, for what is death to a believer ? "

Professor Jebb wrote a singularly happy Greek epitaph upon Gordon, of which the following is a translation : — " Leaving a perpetual remembrance, thou art gone ; in thy death thou wert even such as in thy life, wealth to the poor, hope to the desponding, support to the weak. Thou couldst meet desperate troubles with a spirit that knew not despair, and breathe might into the trembling.

" The Lord of China owes thee thanks for thy

benefits ; the throne of his ancient kingdom hath not been cast down.

"And where the hill unites the divided strength of his streams, a city saw thee long-suffering. A multitude dwelt therein, but thine alone was the valour that guarded it through all that year, when by day and by night thou didst keep watch against the host of the Arabians, who went around it to devour it with spears, thirsting for blood.

"Thy death was not wrought by the God of War, but by the frailties of thy friends. For thy country and for all men God blessed the work of thy hand. Hail, stainless warrior! hail, thrice victorious hero! Thou livest, and shalt teach aftertimes to reverence the counsel of the Everlasting Father."

STATUE ERECTED TO GORDON IN TRAFALGAR SQUARE, LONDON.

The character of Gordon has elicited admiration

from men of all climes, and of all ranks and conditions of life. One of the most remarkable tributes to his magnetic force was that paid by the negro boy Capsune, whom the General rescued from the slave-dealers in 1879. He asked the lady who had charge of him whether she was quite sure that Gordon Pasha still kept his blue eyes, and did she think he could "see all through me now?" Another day he said he was "quite sure Gordon Pasha could see quite well in the dark, because he had the light inside him."

One who knew Gordon well, justly said that it was necessary to know him personally to understand him; for he was so unique, so utterly unlike any one else, that a close friendship was necessary to comprehend fully the greatness and goodness of heart that moved all his actions, even the smallest.

Of course the hero of Khartoum was not a perfect man. He had much to contend with in his own nature, for he was peculiarly one of those in whom the human and Divine elements war against each other strongly. But in contending against the flesh, as his sister remarked, " the indwelling of God enabled him to sustain that conflict which ended only in the death of that flesh. Now the real man is with his much-loved God." If there was dross in Gordon's character, it was less than in that of most men. As for the Bible, it was his constant companion, and his most reverent study. Armed with its consolations, he got very near to Heaven, while as yet the body chained him to Earth.

ABERDEEN: THE UNIVERSITY PRESS

S. W. PARTRIDGE & CO.'S
CATALOGUE

. . OF . .

POPULAR ILLUSTRATED BOOKS.

Classified according to price.

LONDON: S. W. PARTRIDGE & CO., LTD.,
21 & 22, OLD BAILEY, LONDON, E.C.

And of all Booksellers.

10s. net.

The British Battle Fleet : Its Inception and Growth through-out the Centuries. By F. T. Jane, Author of " Fighting Ships," etc. Royal 8vo. 25 Illustrations in three-colour by W. L Wyllie, R.A., and other unique Illustrations in black-and-white.

6s. each.

Large 8vo. Cloth Boards, gilt top.

Captain Brereton Series.

A Sub. of the R.N.R.   A Story of the Great War. By Percy F. Westerman.

The Outlaws of St. Martyn's. A Public-School Story. By Gunby Hadath.

The Dreadnought of the Air ! By Percy F. Westerman, Author of " The Rival Submarines," etc.

King of Ranleigh ! A School Story. By Captain Brereton, Author of " A Boy of the Dominion," etc.

The Last of his Line. A Public-School Story. By Gunby Hadath, Author of " Paying the Price," etc.

Wanted, an English Girl : The Adventure of an English School Girl in Germany. By Dorothea Moore.

The Letter Killeth. By A. C. Inchbold.

5s. each.

" Empire " Library.

Demy 8vo. 432 pages. Illustrations in Colour. Handsomely bound in Cloth Boards, Olivine Edges.

Paying the Price ! A Public-School Story. By Gunby Hadath.

Rosemary, the Rebel ! By Dorothea Moore.

Head of the School. By Harold Avery.

5s. each *(continued)*.

"EMPIRE LIBRARY" *(continued)*.

A Runaway Princess; or, H. R. H. Smith at School. By Dorothea Moore, Author of "A Lady of Mettle," etc.

The Boy Bondsman; or, Under the Lash. By Kent Carr.

In the Mahdi's Grasp. By Geo. Manville Fenn.

"Not Out!" A Public-School Story. By Kent Carr.

Playing the Game! A Story of School Life. By the same Author.

Trapper Dan. A Story of the Backwoods. By Geo. Manville Fenn.

A Lady of Mettle. By Dorothea Moore.

A Wilful Maid. By Evelyn Everett-Green.

"My Book": A Personal Narrative. By Sarah Robinson. Crown 8vo. 288 pages, with more than 300 illustrations. 5s. net.

3s. 6d. net.

Wild Animals of Yesterday and To-day. By Frank Finn, F.Z.S.

The Book of the Wilderness and Jungle. By F. G. Aflalo, F.R.G.S. Demy 8vo. With 12 Illustrations by E. N. Caldwell.

3s. 6d. each.

Large Crown 8vo. Coloured and other illustrations. Cloth Boards, with gilt top.

The Rival Submarines. By Percy F. Westerman, Author of "The Dreadnought of the Air," etc.

"Not Cricket!" A School Story. By Harold Avery.

A Fair Prisoner. A Story of the Great Year. By Morice Gerard.

The Prisoner of the Garret. By Mrs. Baillie Reynolds.

Modern Daughters. By Maria Steuart.

The Opal Hunters; or, The Men of Red Creek Camp. By Robert Macdonald, Author of "The Pearl Lagoons," etc.

The Doings of Dick and Dan: A Book for Boys and Tomboys. By Sir James Yoxall, M.P.

3s. 6d. each *(continued)*.

The Bondage of Riches. By Annie S. Swan.

What Shall it Profit; or, Roden's Choice. By Annie S. Swan.

Just Percy. A Tale of Dicton School. By H. S. Whiting.

Casque and Cowl: A Tale of the French Reformation. By F. M. Cotton Walker.

The Children's Saviour; or, Stories from the Life of Jesus Christ. Told in Fifty-two Chapters. By Mildred Duff. Twelve full-page Coloured Illustrations. Small 4to. 3s. 6d.

The Story of the Bible. Arranged in Simple Style for Young People. Demy 8vo. 620 pages. Eight beautiful pictures in colours, and more than 100 other illustrations. Cloth extra, 3s. 6d. Gilt edges, bevelled boards, 4s. 6d.

Partridge's Children's Annual.

CONDUCTED BY THE EDITOR OF "THE CHILDREN'S FRIEND."

A handsome and attractive production, with cover printed in ten colours and varnished. Pictures in colour on every page throughout. Short stories by all the well-known writers. Paper boards, cloth back, 3s. 6d. Also in cloth boards at 5s.

2s. 6d. each.

" Girls' Imperial Library."

By Popular Authors. Large Crown 8vo. 330 pages. Six Illustrations printed in photo brown. Handsomely bound in Cloth Boards.

(Books marked with an asterisk are also bound with Gilt edges, 3s. each.)

Girls who were Famous Queens. By Kent Carr.

Heart o' Gold; or, The Little Princess. By Katharine Tynan.

A Wayward Girl. By Mrs. Baillie Reynolds.

Pride o' the Morning. By Agnes Giberne.

Tested! By Amy Le Feuvre.

The Girls Next Door. By Christina Gowans Whyte.

Houses of Clay! By Lillias Campbell Davidson.

Under the Wolf's Fell. By Dorothea Moore.

2s. 6d. each *(continued)*.

"GIRLS' IMPERIAL LIBRARY" *(continued)*.

The Girl who Lost Things! A School Story. By L. Tyack.

Nora, the Girl Guide; or, From Tenderfoot to Silver Fish. By A. M. Irvine, Author of the Worst Girl in the School," etc.

*The Worst Girl in the School; or, The Secret Staff. By A. M. Irvine.

*Curiosity Kate! By Florence Bone.

A Wife Worth Winning. By C. E. C. Weigall.

A Lost Inheritance; or, an Earl without an Earldom. By Scott Graham.

*Study Number Eleven: A Tale of Kilton School. By Margaret Kilroy.

*A Daughter of the West: or, Ruth Gwynnett, Schoolmistress. By Morice Gerard.

*The Lucas Girls; or, "The Man of the Family." By Dorothea Moore.

*The Probationer. By A. M. Irvine.

*Margot's Secret; or, The Fourth Form at Victoria College. By Florence Bone.

Far Above Rubies. By C. E. C. Weigall, Author of " A Wife Worth Winning."

*Old Readymoney's Daughter. By L. T. Meade.

*A Girl of the Fourth. A Story for School Girls. By A. M. Irvine.

*Her Little Kingdom. By Laura A. Barter-Snow.

*Evan Grayle's Daughters. By Isabel Suart Robson, Author of "The Fortunes of Eight," etc.

*The Lady of the Forest. By L. T. Meade.

*Cliff House. A Story for School Girls. By A. M. Irvine.

*Carol Carew; or, An Act of Imprudence. By Evelyn Everett-Green. Author of " The Three-Cornered House," etc.

Gladys's Repentance; or, Two Girls and a Fortune. By Edith C. Kenyon.

Ursula; or, A Candidate for the Ministry. By Laura A. Barter-Snow.

A Golden Dawn; or, The Heiress of St. Quentin. By Dorothea Moore.

The Fortunes of Eight; or, The House in Harford Place. By Isabel Suart Robson.

Through Surging Waters. By H. Davies.

The " True Grit " Series.

Large Crown 8vo.   320 pages.   Fully Illustrated.   Handsomely Bound in Cloth Boards.

(Books marked with an asterisk are also bound with Gilt edges, 3s. each.)

The Pearl Lagoons ; or, The Lost Chief. A Story of Adventure in the South Seas. By Robert Macdonald.

The Boys' Book of the Navy. By Cuthbert Hadden.

Runners of Contraband. By Tom Bevan.

The Common Beetles of our Countryside. By W. E. Sharp, F.E.S.

Never Say Die ! A Public-School Story. By Gunby Hadath. Author of " Paying the Price," etc.

Doughty Deeds of Derring-Do. The Story of Chivalry. By Hammond Hall.

By Seashore, Wood and Moorland. By Edward Step, F.L.S., Author of " Wayside Flowers," etc.

With Bandit and Turk. By Tom Bevan, Author of " Trapped in Tripoli ! " etc.

Jack Rollock's Adventures. By Hugh St. Leger.

*Trapped in Tripoli ! By Tom Bevan, Author of " Runners of Contraband," etc.

*Talford's Last Term. By Harold Avery.

*Out with the Buccaneers ; or, The Treasure of the Snake. By Tom Bevan.

*The Castaways of Disappointment Island. By H. Escott-Inman

*Cap'n Nat's Treasure : A Tale of Old Liverpool. By Robert Leighton.

*The Secret Men. By Tom Bevan.

Rambles among the Flowers. By T. Carreras. With coloured plates and other illustrations.

*By Mountain, Moorland, River, and Shore. By T. Carreras. With coloured and many other Illustrations.

*By Summer Seas and Flowery Fields. By T. Carreras.

*The Wild Life of our Land. By T. Carreras. Uniform with the above.

*Nature Walks and Talks. By T. Carreras. Large crown 8vo. Many Illustrations. Cloth boards.

*Jungle and Stream ; or, The Adventures of Two Boys in Siam. By Geo. Manville Fenn.

*" Sandfly " ; or, In the Indian Days. By F. B. Forester.

The Boy's Book of the Sea. By W. H. Simmonds.

2s. 6d. each (*continued*).

THE "TRUE GRIT" SERIES (*continued*).

A Boy of the First Empire. By Elbridge S. Brooks.

The Boy's Life of Nelson. By J. Cuthbert Hadden. Large Crown 8vo. 300 pages. Beautiful coloured frontispiece, and eight illustrations on art paper.

*True Grit: A Story of Adventure in West Africa. By Harold Bindloss. Six Illustrations.

The Children's Treasury. Compiled and Edited by Ethel Lindsay. Charmingly illustrated. 2s. 6d. **net.**

The Golliwog News. A Story for Children. By Philip and Fay Inchfawn. Large Crown 8vo. 12 illustrations by T. C. Smith.
A miniature copy of a "Golliwog Newspaper" is given with each book.

The Pilgrim's Progress. By John Bunyan. Beautifully bound in cloth boards, and illustrated with more than 60 full-page and other engravings in both colour and black-and-white. Handsome cloth bound, 2s. 6d.; full gilt edges, 3s. 6d.

Come, Break your Fast: Daily Meditations for a Year. By Rev. Mark Guy Pearse. Large Crown 8vo. 554 pages. With Portrait. Cloth boards.

A Young Man's Mind. By J. A. Hammerton. Crown 8vo. Cloth extra, gilt top.

The Missionary Prospect. With a Survey of the World's Missions. By Canon H. Robinson. Large Crown 8vo. Cloth boards, 2s. 6d. **net.**

The Romance of Bible Study. An Exposition of the Method, a Demonstration of the Power, and a Revelation of the Joy of true Bible Reading. By Rev. Martin Anstey, M.A. 2s. 6d. **net.**

Our Rulers from William the Conqueror to Edward VII. By J. Alexander. Foolscap 4to. Cloth gilt.

The Great Siberian Railway: What I saw on my Journey. By Dr. F. E. Clark. Crown 8vo. 213 pages. Sixty-five first-class Illustrations on art paper, and a Map. Handsomely bound.

Brought to Jesus: A Bible Picture Book for Little Readers.

Bible Pictures and Stories: Old and New Testament.

Victoria: Her Life and Reign. By Alfred E. Knight.

2s. 6d. each (*continued*).

Ferrar Fenton's Translations of the Holy Scriptures in Modern English.

Cloth, 2s. 6d. each net. *Paste Grain, 3s. 6d. each* net.

Vol.   I.—The Five Books of Moses.
Vol. II.—The History of Israel.
Vol. III.—The Books of the Prophets.
Vol. IV.—The Psalms, Solomon, and Sacred Writers.
Vol. V.—The New Testament.
The Complete Bible in Modern English, Incorporating the above five volumes. Cloth extra, gilt top. 7s. 6d. net. Paste Grain, 12s. 6d. net.

By Dr. A. C. DIXON.

Large Crown 8vo. Cloth, gilt. 2s. net.

Present Day Life and Religion.
The Glories of the Cross.
The Bright Side of Life.
Back to the Bible.

2s. each.

"*Geo. Manville Fenn*" *Series.*

A new issue of the most popular stories by this prince of writers for Boys. Exceptional value is shown in these volumes.

The Crystal Hunters.	Sappers and Miners.
In Honour's Cause.	Cormorant Crag.
First in the Field.	
Steve Young.	
Rob Harlow's Adventures.	
The Adventures of Don Lavington.	

2s. each.

The Home Library.

Crown 8vo.   320 pages.   Handsome Cloth Covers.   Fully Illustrated.
(Books marked with an asterisk are also bound with Gilt edges, 2s. 6d. each)

Norah's Victory; or, Saved through Suffering. By Laura A. Barter-Snow. Author of " Harold," etc.

2s. each *(continued)*.

THE HOME LIBRARY *(continued)*.

In the Misty Seas. By H. Bindloss.
The Heart of Una Sackville. By Mrs. Geo. de Horne Vaizey.
A Girl in a Thousand. By Edith Kenyon.
The Singer of the Kootenay. By R. E. Knowles.
The Children of the Crag. By Amy Whipple.
A Strong Man's Love. By David Lyall.
Those Berkeley Girls. By Lillias Campbell Davidson.
A Girl's Stronghold. By Eliza F. Pollard.
Done and Dared in Old France. By Deborah Alcock.
A Lion of Wessex. By Tom Bevan.
A Compleat Sea Cook. By Frank T. Bullen.
The Salvage of a Sailor. By Frank T. Bullen.
Under Wolfe's Flag. By Rowland Walker.
The Splendid Stars. By Florence E. Bone.
The Three-Cornered House. By Evelyn Everett-Green.
A Study in Gold ! By Grace Pettman.
*Who Conquers? or, A Schoolboy's Honour. By Florence Bone.
From School to Castle. By Charlotte Murray.
*Miss Elizabeth's Family. By Kent Carr.
*Hope Glynne's Awakening. By Jessie Goldsmith Cooper.
*The Call of Honour. By C. F. Argyll-Saxby.
*Agnes Dewsbury. By Laura A. Barter-Snow.
A Lady of High Degree. By Jennie Chappell.
Comrades Three ! A Story of the Canadian Prairies. By Argyll-Saxby.
The Fighting Lads of Devon. By Wm. Murray Graydon.
*A Little Bundle of Mischief. By Grace Carlton.
*A Gentleman of England. By E. F. Pollard.
*Three Chums ; or, The Little Blue Heart. By E. M. Stooke.
*Helena's Dower. By Eglanton Thorne.
*True unto Death ; A Story of Russian Life. By E. F. Pollard.
Love Conquereth. By Charlotte Murray.
White Ivory and Black, and other Stories of Adventure by Sea and Land. By Tom Bevan, E. Harcourt Burrage, and John Higginson.
Brave Brothers; or, Young Sons of Providence. By E. M. Stooke.
*The Moat House ; or, Celia's Deceptions. By Eleanora H. Stooke.
The Better Part. By Annie S. Swan.

2s. each (*continued*).

THE HOME LIBRARY (*continued*).

Lights and Shadows of Forster Square. By Rev. E. H. Sugden, M.A.

Morning Dew-Drops : A Temperance Text Book. By Clara Lucas Balfour.

Mark Desborough's Vow. By Annie S. Swan.

My Dogs in the Northland. By Egerton R. Young. 288 pages.

The Strait Gate. By Annie S. Swan.

Alfred the Great : The Father of the English. By Jesse Page.

Library of Standard Works by Famous Authors.

Crown 8vo.   Bound in Handsome Cloth Boards.   Well Illustrated.

(Books marked with an asterisk are also bound with Gilt edges, 2s. 6d. each).

Tales from Shakespeare. By Mary and Charles Lamb.

Daisy. A Sequel to "Melbourne House." By Elizabeth Wetherell.

Daisy in the Field. By the same Author.

The Wonder Book and Tanglewood Tales. By Nathaniel Hawthorne.

The Young Fur Traders. By R. M. Ballantyne.

A Book of Golden Deeds. By Charlotte Yonge.

*Julian Home. By F. W. Farrar.

Roland Yorke. By Mrs. Henry Wood.

Lorna Doone. By R. D. Blackmore.

*Harold : The Last of the Saxon Kings. By Bulwer Lytton.

Mrs. Overtheway's Remembrances. By Juliana Horatia Ewing.

*Eric : or, Little by Little. By F. W. Farrar.

*St. Winifred's. By the same Author.

The Fairy Book : Fairy Stories Re-told Anew. By Mrs. Craik, Author of "John Halifax, Gentleman."

*Adam Bede. By George Eliot.

*The Schonberg-Cotta Family. By Mrs. Rundle Charles.

Reminiscences of a Highland Parish. By Norman Macleod.

*From Log Cabin to White House ; The Story of President Garfield. By W. M. Thayer.

The Children of the New Forest. By Captain Marryat.

The Starling. By Norman Macleod.

*Hereward the Wake. By Charles Kingsley.

The Heroes. By Charles Kingsley.

2s. each *(continued)*.

LIBRARY of STANDARD WORKS by FAMOUS AUTHORS *(contd.)*

The Channings. By Mrs. Henry Wood.
Ministering Children. By M. L. Charlesworth.
Ministering Children : A Sequel. By the same Author.
The Water Babies. A Fairy Tale for a Land Baby. By Charles Kingsley.
*Hans Andersen's Fairy Tales.
Coral Island. By R. M. Ballantyne.
Nettie's Mission. By Alice Gray.
Home Influence : A Tale for Mothers. By Grace Aguilar.
The Gorilla Hunters. By R. M. Ballantyne.
*What Katy Did. By Susan Coolidge.
Peter the Whaler. By W. H. G. Kingston.
Melbourne House. By Susan Warner.
*The Lamplighter. By Miss Cummins.
*Grimm's Fairy Tales.
The Swiss Family Robinson : Adventures on a Desert Island.
*Tom Brown's Schooldays. By an Old Boy.
*Little Women and Good Wives. By Louisa M. Alcott.
The Wide, Wide World. By Susan Warner.
Danesbury House. By Mrs. Henry Wood.
Stepping Heavenward. By E. Prentiss.
John Halifax, Gentleman. By Mrs. Craik.
*Life and Adventures of Robinson Crusoe. By Daniel Defoe.
Naomi; or, The Last Days of Jerusalem. By Mrs. Webb.
*The Pilgrim's Progress. By John Bunyan.
Uncle Tom's Cabin. By Harriet Beecher Stowe.
Westward Ho! By Charles Kingsley.

" *Great Deeds* " *Series.*

Large Crown 8vo. 320 pages. Full of Illustrations. Handsomely bound in Cloth Boards. 2s. each. (Also with Gilt edges, 2s. 6d. each.)

Great-Heart Lincoln. By W. F. Aitken.
Stirring Sea Fights. By J. Cuthbert Hadden.
'Mid Snow and Ice. Stories of Peril in Polar Seas. By C. D. Michael.
Heroes of the Darkness. By J. Bernard Mannix.
Stories of Self-Help. By John Alexander.

2s. each *(continued)*.

"GREAT DEEDS" SERIES *(continued)*.

Famous Boys : A Book of Brave Endeavour. By C. D. Michael.

Noble Workers : Sketches of the Life and Work of Nine Noble Women. By Jennie Chappell.

Heroes of our Empire : Gordon, Clive, Warren Hastings, Havelock and Lawrence.

Heroes who have Won their Crown : David Livingstone and John Williams.

Great Works by Great Men. By F. M. Holmes.

Brave Deeds for British Boys. By C. D. Michael.

Two Great Explorers : The Lives of Fridtjof Nansen and Sir Henry M. Stanley.

Heroes of the Land and Sea : Firemen and their Exploits, and the Lifeboat.

Heroic Leaders : Great Saints of British Christianity. By Dinsdale T. Young. 2s. net.

The Story of Jesus. For Little Children. By Mrs. G. E. Morton. Large 8vo. 340 pages. Eight pictures in best style of colour-work, and many other Illustrations. Handsomely bound in cloth boards.

Love, Courtship, and Marriage. By Rev. F. B. Meyer, B.A. Crown 8vo. 152 pages. Embellished cloth cover, 2s. net. Full Gilt Edges, 2s. 6d net.

The Influence of the Press : Its Power and its Weakness. By R. A. Scott-James. 2s. net.

1s. 6d. each.

The Up-to-Date Library

Of Thick Crown 8vo. Volumes. 320 pages. Many Illustrations. Cloth Boards.

Molly. By H. E. Colvile.

"The Little Missis." By Charlotte Skinner.

Uncle Joshua's Heiress. By L. C. Davidson.

The Flowers of Fairyland. By Edith King-Hall.

Smoking Flax. By Silas K. Hocking.

1s. 6d. each *(continued)*.

THE UP-TO-DATE LIBRARY *(continued)*.

(Books marked with an asterisk are also bound with gilt edges, 2s. each.)

Old Wenyon's Will. By John Ackworth.

Neta Lyall. By Flora E. Berry.

The White Dove. By E. F. Pollard.

The Yellow Shield. By W. Johnston.

Roger the Ranger. By E. F. Pollard.

Crag Island; or, The Mystery of Val Stanlock. By W. Murray Graydon.

A Girl's Battle. By Lillias Campbell Davidson.

Edwin, the Boy Outlaw. By J. Frederick Hodgetts

Stuart's Choice; or, Castleton's "Prep." By Charlotte Murray.

*One of the Tenth. By William Johnston.

Wardlaugh; or, Workers Together. By Charlotte Murray.

More than Money! By A. St. John Adcock.

Norman's Nugget. By J. Macdonald Oxley.

*A Desert Scout: A Tale of Arabi's Revolt. By Wm. Johnston.

The Red Mountain of Alaska. By Willis Boyd Allen.

Coral: A Sea Waif and Her Friends. By Charlotte Murray.

Robert Aske: A Story of the Reformation. By E. F. Pollard.

The Lion City of Africa. By Willis Boyd Allen.

The Spanish Maiden: A Story of Brazil. By Emma E. Hornibrook.

The Boy from Cuba. A School Story. By Walter Rhoades.

*Through Grey to Gold. By Charlotte Murray.

*Dorothy's Training. By Jennie Chappell.

Manco, the Peruvian Chief. By W. H. G. Kingston.

*Muriel Malone; or, From Door to Door. By Charlotte Murray.

Her Saddest Blessing. By Jennie Chappell.

A Trio of Cousins. By Mrs. G. E. Morton.

Mick Tracy, the Irish Scripture Reader.

Without a Thought; or Dora's Discipline. By Jennie Chappell.

Edith Oswald; or, Living for Others. By Jane M. Kippen.

A Village Story. By Mrs. G. E. Morton.

The Eagle Cliff. By R. M. Ballantyne.

1s. 6d. each (*continued*).

THE UP-TO-DATE LIBRARY (*continued*).

The Slave Raiders of Zanzibar. By E. Harcourt Burrage.
Avice. A Story of Imperial Rome. By E. F. Pollard.
The King's Daughter. By "Pansy."
Three People. By "Pansy."
*The Young Moose Hunters. By C. A. Stephens.
*Eaglehurst Towers. By Emma Marshall.

Uncle Mac, the Missionary. By Jean Perry. Six Illustrations by Wal. Paget on art paper. Cloth boards.
Chilgoopie the Glad : A Story of Korea and her Children. By Jean Perry. Eight Illustrations on art paper. Cloth boards.
The Man in Grey ; or, More about Korea. By Jean Perry.
Queen Alexandra : the Nation's Pride. By Mrs. C. N. Williamson. Crown 8vo. Tastefully bound. 1s. 6d **net**.
William McKinley : Private and President. By Thos. Cox Meech. Crown 8vo. 160 pages, with Portrait. 1s. 6d. **net**.
Wellington : the Record of a Great Military Career. By A. E. Knight. Crown 8vo. Cloth gilt, with Portrait. 1s. 6d. **net**.

The British Boys' Library.

Fully Illustrated. Crown 8vo. 168 pages. Cloth extra.

Rupert's Resolve. By Laura A. Barter-Snow.
Barney Boy. By the same Author.
The Yellow Pup : A Story for Boys. By Evelyn Everett-Green.
The Crew of the Rectory. By M. B. Manwell.
The King's Scouts. By William R. A. Wilson.
General John : A Story for Boy Scouts. By Evelyn Everett-Green.
Through Flame and Flood. Stories of Heroism on Land and Sea. By C. D. Michael.
Never Beaten! A Story of a Boy's Adventures in Canada. By E. Harcourt Burrage, Author of "Gerard Mastyn," etc.
Noble Deeds: Stories of Peril and Heroism. Edited by C. D. Michael.

1s. 6d. each (*continued*).

THE BRITISH BOYS' LIBRARY (*continued*).

Armour Bright. The Story of a Boy's Battles. By Lucy Taylor.

Brown A1; or, A Stolen Holiday. By E. M. Stooke.

Robin the Rebel. By H. Louisa Bedford.

The British Girls' Library.

Fully Illustrated. Crown 8vo. 160 pages. Cloth extra.

"Meddlesome Mattie." By A. Miall.

An Unpopular Schoolgirl. By Bertha Mary Fisher.

The Girls of St. Ursula's. A Story of School Life. By M. B. Manwell.

The Little Heroine. By Brenda Girvin.

Alison's Quest; or, The Mysterious Treasure. By Florence E. Bone.

Little Gladwise. The Story of a Waif. By Nellie Cornwall.

A Family of Nine! By E. C. Phillips.

Alice and the White Rabbit: Their Trips Round about London. By Brenda Girvin.

Friendless Felicia: or, A Little City Sparrow. By Eleanora H. Stooke.

Keziah in Search of a Friend. By Noel Hope.

Granny's Girls. By M. B. Manwell.

The Gipsy Queen. By Emma Leslie.

Book Lover's Library.

With beautiful coloured frontispiece, illustrated title page and other illustrations. Art Binding. 1s. 6d. each, net.

THE WONDERBOOK AND TANGLE-WOOD TALES.

THE YOUNG FUR-TRADERS.

LAMB'S TALES FROM SHAKE-PEARE.

DAISY.

DAISY IN THE FIELD.

JULIAN HOME. By F. W. Farrar.

ROLAND YORKE. By Mrs. Henry Wood.

LORNA DOONE. By R. D. Blackmore.

A BOOK OF GOLDEN DEEDS. By Charlotte Yonge.

THE LITTLE DUKE. By the same Author.

SELF-HELP. By Samuel Smiles.

HAROLD; or, The Last of the Saxon Kings. By Bulwer Lytton.

1s. 6d. each (*continued*).

BOOK LOVER'S LIBRARY (*continued*).   1s. 6d. net.

ERIC; or, Little by Little. By F. W. Farrar.

ST. WINIFREDS. By the same Author.

THE HEROES. By Charles Kingsley.

ALICE IN WONDERLAND. By Lewis Carroll.

JOHN HALIFAX, GENTLEMAN. By Mrs. Craik.

GRIMM'S FAIRY TALES.

HANS ANDERSEN'S FAIRY TALES.

WESTWARD HO! By Charles Kingsley.

TOM BROWN'S SCHOOLDAYS.

LITTLE WOMEN AND GOOD WIVES. By Louisa M. Alcott.

HEREWARD THE WAKE. By Charles Kingsley.

UNCLE TOM'S CABIN. By H. B. Stowe.

Popular Missionary Biographies.

Large Crown 8vo.   160 pages.   Cloth extra.   Fully Illustrated.

J. G. Paton : The Man and His Mission. By C. D. Michael.

Timothy Richard, D.D., the Apostle of Literature in China. By Rev. B. Reeve.

George Augustus Selwyn : The Pioneer Bishop of New Zealand. By Frank W. Boreham.

James Hannington : Bishop and Martyr. By C. D. Michael.

Two Lady Missionaries in Tibet : Miss Annie R. Taylor and Dr. Susie Rijnhart Moyes. By Isabel S. Robson.

Dr. Laws of Livingstonia. By Rev. J. Johnston.

Grenfell of Labrador. By Rev. J. Johnston.

Johan G. Oncken : His Life and Work. By Rev. J. Hunt Cooke.

James Chalmers, Missionary and Explorer of Rarotonga and New Guinea. By William Robson.

Griffith John, Founder of the Hankow Mission, Central China. By William Robson.

Robert Morrison : The Pioneer of Chinese Missions. By William J. Townsend.

Captain Allen Gardiner : Sailor and Saint. By Jesse Page.

The Congo for Christ : The Story of the Congo Mission. By Rev. J. B. Myers.

David Brainerd, the Apostle to the North-American Indians. By Jesse Page, F.R.G.S.

David Livingstone. By Arthur Montefiore-Brice.

John Williams : The Martyr Missionary of Polynesia. By Rev. James Ellis.

Lady Missionaries in Foreign Lands. By Mrs. E. R. Pitman.

Missionary Heroines in Eastern Lands. By Mrs. E. R. Pitman.

1s. 6d. each (*continued*).

POPULAR MISSIONARY BIOGRAPHIES (*continued*).

Henry Martyn : His Life and Labours. By Jesse Page.

Robert Moffat : The Missionary Hero of Kuruman. By David J. Deane.

Samuel Crowther : The Slave Boy who became Bishop of the Niger. By Jesse Page, F.R.G.S.

Bishop Patteson : The Martyr of Melanesia. By same Author.

William Carey : The Shoemaker who became the Father and Founder of Modern Missions. By Rev. J. B. Myers.

John Wesley. By Rev. Arthur Walters.

From Kafir Kraal to Pulpit : The Story of Tiyo Soga, First Ordained Preacher of the Kafir Race. By Rev. H. T. Cousins.

James Calvert ; or, From Dark to Dawn in Fiji. By R. Vernon.

Thomas J. Comber : Missionary Pioneer to the Congo. By Rev. J. B. Myers.

The Christianity of the Continent. By Jesse Page, F.R.G.S.

Popular Biographies.

Large Crown 8vo. Cloth Boards. Fully Illustrated.

Women of Worth. Sketches of the Lives of the Queen of Roumania ("Carmen Sylva"), Frances Power Cobbe, Mrs. J. R. Bishop, and Mrs. Bramwell Booth. By Jennie Chappell.

Women who have Worked and Won. The Life Story of Mrs. Spurgeon, Mrs. Booth-Tucker, F. R. Havergal, and Ramabai. By Jennie Chappell.

Noble Work by Noble Women : Sketches of the Lives of the Baroness Burdett-Coutts, Lady Henry Somerset, Mrs. Sarah Robinson, Mrs. Fawcett, and Mrs. Gladstone. By Jennie Chappell.

Four Noble Women and their Work : Sketches of the Life and Work of Frances Willard, Agnes Weston, Sister Dora, and Catherine Booth. By Jennie Chappell.

Florence Nightingale : The Wounded Soldier's Friend. By Eliza F. Pollard.

B

1s. 6d. each (*continued*).

POPULAR BIOGRAPHIES (*continued*).

Four Heroes of India. Clive, Warren Hastings, Havelock, Lawrence. **By F. M. Holmes.**

General Gordon : The Christian Soldier and Hero. **By G. Barnett Smith.**

Two Noble Lives : John Wicliffe, the Morning Star of the Reformation ; and Martin Luther, the Reformer. **By David J. Deane. 208 pages.**

Heroes and Heroines of the Scottish Covenanters. By **J. Meldrum Dryerre, LL.B., F.R.G.S.**

John Knox and the Scottish Reformation. By G. **Barnett Smith.**

George Müller : The Modern Apostle of Faith. By **Fred G. Warne.**

John Bright : Apostle of Free Trade. By Jesse Page, F.R.G.S.

Philip Melancthon : The Wittemberg Professor and Theologian of the Reformation. **By David J. Deane.**

The Marquess of Salisbury : His Inherited Characteristics, **Political Principles, and Personality.** By W. F. Aitken.

Joseph Parker, D.D. : His Life and Ministry. By Albert **Dawson.**

Hugh Price Hughes. By Rev. J. Gregory Mantle.

R. J. Campbell, M.A. ; Minister of the City Temple, London. **By Charles T. Bateman.**

Dr. Barnardo : "The Foster-Father of Nobody's Children." By **Rev. J. H. Batt.**

W. Robertson Nicoll, LL.D. ; Editor and Preacher. By Jane **Stoddart.**

F. B. Meyer : His Life and Work. By M. Jennie Street.

John Clifford, M.A., B.Sc., LL.D., D.D. By Chas. T. Bateman.

1s. 6d. each *(continued)*.

<u>POPULAR BIOGRAPHIES</u> *(continued)*.

Thirty Years in the East End. A Marvellous Story of Mission Work. By W. Francis Aitken.

Alexander Maclaren, D.D. : The Man and His Message. By Rev. John C. Carlile.

Lord Milner. By W. B. Luke.

Lord Rosebery, Imperialist. By J. A. Hammerton.

Joseph Chamberlain : A Romance of Modern Politics. By Arthur Mee.

Picture Books.

Size, 10¾ × 8½ inches. With 6 charming coloured plates, and beautifully printed in colours throughout. For bulk and quality these books are exceptional. Handsome coloured covers, with cloth backs. 1s. 6d. each.

Tell Me a Tale.

Pets and Playmates.

1s. each.

First Steps to Nursing. A Handbook for Nursing Candidates. By Mabel Cave. 1s. net.

The Chief Scout : The Life of Lieut.-Gen. Sir Robert Baden-Powell. By W. Francis Aitken.

Golden Words for Every Day. By M. Jennie Street. 1s.

Novelties, and How to Make Them : Hints and Helps in providing occupation for Children's Classes. Compiled by Mildred Duff. Full of Illustrations. Cloth boards, 1s.

In Defence of the Faith : The Old Better than the New. By Rev. F. B. Meyer. Cloth Boards, 1s.

Ingatherings : A Dainty Book of Beautiful Thoughts. Compiled by E. Agar. Cloth boards, 1s. net. Paper covers, 6d. net.

The New Cookery of Unproprietary Foods. By Eustace Miles, M.A. 192 pages. 1s. net.

1s. each (*continued*).

Books for Christian Workers.

Large Crown 16mo.   128 pages.   Chastely bound in Cloth Boards.   1s. each.

The Home Messages of Jesus. By Charlotte Skinner.

Deeper Yet :   Meditations for the Quiet Hour.   By Clarence E. Eberman.

Royal and Loyal.   Thoughts on the Two-fold Aspect of the Christian Life. By Rev. W. H. Griffith-Thomas.

The Overcoming Life. By Rev. E. W. Moore.

Some Deeper Things. By Rev. F. B. Meyer.

Steps to the Blessed Life. By Rev. F. B. Meyer.

Daybreak in the Soul. By Rev. E. W. Moore.

The Temptation of Christ. By C. Arnold Healing, M.A.

One Shilling Reward Books.

Fully Illustrated.   Crown 8vo.   128 pages.   Cloth extra.

" Tops !"   A Story of a Poor Waif.   By Jessie Challacombe.

A Schoolboy's Honour ; or, The Lost Pigeons. By Ethel Lindsay.

Iredale Minor.   A School Story for Boys.   By Meredith Fletcher.

Kitty's Enemy ; or, The Boy next Door. By Eleanora H. Stooke.

Crackers. The Story of a Little Monkey. By May Wynne.

Tommy and the Owl. By Evelyn Everett-Green.

A Fair Reward : The Story of a Prize. By Jennie Chappell.

Jeff's Charge : A Story of London Life. By Charles Herbert.

The Making of Ursula. By Dorothea Moore.

Jimmy : The Tale of a Little Black Bear. By May Wynne.

"Tubby" ; or, Right about Face. By J. Howard Brown.

1s. each *(continued)*.

ONE SHILLING REWARD BOOKS *(continued)*.

Alan's Puzzle; or, The Bag of Gold.   By F. M. Holmes.

Billy's Hero; or, The Valley of Gold.   A Story of Canadian Adventure.   By Marjorie L. C. Pickthall.

The Whitedown Chums.   By Jas. H. Brown.

Sweet Nancy.   By L. T. Meade.

All Play and No Work.   By Harold Avery.

Always Happy; or, The Story of Helen Keller.   By Jennie Chappell.

Harold; or, Two Died for Me.   By Laura A. Barter-Snow.

Indian Life in the Great North-West.   By Egerton R. Young.

Jack the Conqueror; or, Difficulties Overcome.   By Mrs. C. E. Bowen.

Lost in the Backwoods.   By Edith C. Kenyon.

The Little Woodman and his Dog Cæsar.   By Mrs. Sherwood.

Roy's Sister; or, His Way and Hers.   By M. B. Manwell.

George & Co.; or, The Chorister of St. Anselm's.   By Spencer T. Gibb.

Ruth's Roses.   By Laura A. Barter-Snow.

Sunshine and Snow.   By Harold Bindloss.

True Stories of Brave Deeds.   By Mabel Bowler.

Paul the Courageous.   By Mabel Quiller-Couch.

The Adventures of Ji.   By G. E. Farrow, Author of "The Wallypug of Why."

A Mysterious Voyage; or, The Adventures of a Dodo.   By G. E. Farrow.

1s. each (*continued*).

Attractive Picture Books.

Coloured Frontispiece and numerous other illustrations. Handsomely bound in paper boards. Covers printed in 10 colours and varnished.

Off and away.

Chickabiddies' Picture Book.

Happy All Day !

Smiles and Dimples.

Dollies' School.

Sunny Days !

Pictures from Playland.

My Dollies' A. B. C.

Holiday Hours in Animal Land.

Animal Antics.

In Animal Land with Louis Wain.

Feed My Lambs.

Old Testament Heroes.

The Life of Jesus.

Bible Pictures and Stories. Old Testament.

Bible Pictures and Stories. New Testament.

1s. net.

Popular " Library " Series.

A Daughter of the West. By Morice Gerard.

The Prisoner of the Garret. By Mrs. Baillie Reynolds.

A Gentleman of England. By E. F. Pollard.

A Lost Inheritance. By Scott Graham.

What shall it Profit ? By Annie S. Swan.

Smoking Flax. By Silas K. Hocking.

1s. each net.

Crown 8vo. Stiff Paper Covers, 1s. each net. Cloth Boards, 1s. 6d. each net. (Not Illustrated).

Partridge's Children's Reciter.

Partridge's Temperance Reciter.

Partridge's Reciter of Sacred and Religious Pieces.

Partridge's Popular Reciter. Old Favourites and New.

Partridge's Humorous Reciter.

1s. each (*continued*).

Cheap Reprints of Popular Books for the Young.

Crown 8vo. 160 pages. Illustrated. Cloth Boards, 1s. each.

Salome's Burden. By E. H. Stooke.

Success! By C. D. Michael.

Dick's Daring. By A. H. Biggs.

Runaway Rollo. By E. M. Stooke.

The Tender Light of Home. By Florence Willmot.

Missionary Heroes. By C. D. Michael.

Nearly Lost, but Dearly Won. By Rev. T. P. Wilson, M.A.

Well Done! Stories of Brave Endeavour. By C. D. Michael.

The Pigeon's Cave. A Story of the Great Orme. By J. S. Fletcher.

Heroines: True Tales of Brave Women. By C. D. Michael.

The Canal Boy who Became President. By F. T. Gammon.

Zillah, the Little Dancing Girl. By Mrs. Hugh St. Leger.

The Lads of Kingston. By J. Capes Story.

Jack, the Story of a Scapegrace. By E. M. Bryant.

Patsie's Bricks. By L. S. Mead.

Kathleen; or, A Maiden's Influence. By Julia Hack.

Her Bright To-morrow. By Laura A. Barter-Snow.

Patsy's Schooldays; or, The Mystery Baby. By Alice M. Page.

Dick's Chum. By M. A. Paull.

Mousey; or, Cousin Robert's Treasure. By E. H. Stooke.

Marigold's Fancies. By L. E. Tiddeman.

The Thane of the Dean. By Tom Bevan.

Nature's Mighty Wonders. By Rev. Richard Newton.

Hubert Ellerdale. By W. Oak Rhind.

The Maid of the Storm. By Nellie Cornwall.

Heroes All! A Book of Brave Deeds. By C. D. Michael.

The Old Red Schoolhouse. By Frances H. Wood.

Christabel's Influence. By J. Goldsmith Cooper.

Deeds of Daring. By C. D. Michael.

Everybody's Friend. By Evelyn Everett-Green.

Vic: A Book of Animal Stories. By A. C. Fryer, Ph.D., F.S.A.

Nella; or, Not My Own. By Jessie Goldsmith Cooper.

Blossom and Blight. By M. A. Paull.

Aileen. By Laura A. Barter-Snow.

A Candle Lighted by the Lord. By Mrs. E. Ross.

1s. each (*continued*).

CHEAP REPRINTS OF POPULAR BOOKS FOR THE YOUNG.

(*continued*).

Alice Western's Blessing. By Ruth Lamb.

Marigold. By Mrs. L. T. Meade.

Jack's Heroism. By Edith C. Kenyon.

The Little Princess of Tower Hill. By L. T. Meade.

Ellerslie House : A Book for Boys. By Emma Leslie.

Like a Little Candle; or, Bertrand's Influence. By Mrs. Haycraft.

The Dairyman's Daughter. By Legh Richmond.

Bible Jewels. By Rev. Dr. Newton.

Bible Wonders. By the same Author.

The Pilgrim's Progress. By John Bunyan. 416 pages. Eight coloured and 46 other Illustrations.

Our Duty to Animals. By Mrs. C. Bray.

Everyone's Library.

A re-issue of Standard Works in a cheap form, containing from 320 to 500 pages, printed in the best style, with Illustrations on art paper, and tastefully bound in Cloth Boards. 1s. each.

Tales from Shakespeare. By Mary and Charles Lamb.

Daisy. By Elizabeth Wetherell.

Daisy in the Field. By the same Author.

The Wonder Book and Tanglewood Tales. By Nathaniel Hawthorne.

The Young Fur Traders. By R. M. Ballantyne.

John Ploughman's Talk. By C. H. Spurgeon.

Julian Home. By F. W. Farrar.

Roland Yorke. By Mrs. Henry Wood.

Lorna Doone. By R. D. Blackmore.

The Little Duke. By Charlotte Yonge.

A Book of Golden Deeds. By the same Author.

Nettie's Mission. By Alice Gray.

Harold : The Last of the Saxon Kings. By Bulwer Lytton.

Mrs. Overtheway's Remembrances. By Juliana Horatia Ewing.

Self Help : Illustrations of Character and Conduct. By Samuel Smiles.

Eric : or, Little by Little. By F. W. Farrar.

St. Winifred's. By the same Author.

The Fairy Book : Fairy Stories Retold Anew. By Mrs. Craik, Author of "John Halifax, Gentleman."

1s. each *(continued)*.

EVERYONE'S LIBRARY *(continued)*.

Ben Hur. By Lew Wallace.
Adam Bede. By George Eliot.
The Schonberg-Cotta Family. By Mrs. Rundle Charles.
Reminiscences of a Highland Parish. By Norman Macleod.
The Strait Gate. By Annie S. Swan.
Mark Desborough's Vow. By Annie S. Swan.
Better Part. By the same Author.
From Log Cabin to White House. By W. M. Thayer.
The Gorilla Hunters. By R. M. Ballantyne.
Naomi; or, The Last Days of Jerusalem. By Mrs. Webb.
The Starling. By Norman Macleod.
The Children of the New Forest. By Captain Marryat.
Danesbury House. By Mrs. Henry Wood.
Granny's Wonderful Chair. By Frances Browne.
Hereward the Wake. By Charles Kingsley.
The Heroes. By Charles Kingsley.
Ministering Children. By M. L. Charlesworth.
Ministering Children : A Sequel. By the same Author.
Peter the Whaler. By W. H. G. Kingston.
The Channings. By Mrs. Henry Wood.
Melbourne House. By Susan Warner.
Alice in Wonderland. By Lewis Carroll.
The Lamplighter. By Miss Cummins.
What Katy Did. By Susan Coolidge.
Stepping Heavenward. By E. Prentiss.
Westward Ho! By Charles Kingsley.
The Water Babies. By the same Author.
The Swiss Family Robinson.
Grimm's Fairy Tales. By the Brothers Grimm.
The Coral Island. By R. M. Ballantyne.
Hans Andersen's Fairy Tales.
John Halifax, Gentleman. By Mrs. Craik.
Little Women and Good Wives. By Louisa M. Alcott.
Tom Brown's Schooldays. By an Old Boy.
The Wide, Wide World. By Susan Warner.
Life and Adventures of Robinson Crusoe. By Daniel Defoe.
Uncle Tom's Cabin. By H. B. Stowe.
The Old Lieutenant and His Son. By Norman Macleod.

1s. each net.

The Boys' Adventure Series.

A new series of books for boys, of remarkable value. There are from 320 to 416 pages in each book. The attractiveness of the series is enhanced by the inclusion of three-colour illustrations and an interest-compelling wrapper. **1s. net.**

Jack Rollock's Adventures.

The Eagle Cliff. By R. M. Ballantyne.

Comrades Three ! By Argyll Saxby.

Trapper Dan. By Manville Fenn.

Out with the Buccaneers. By Tom Bevan.

The Indian Vengeance. By F. B. Forester.

The Castaways of Disappointment Island. By H. Escott Inman.

Cap'n Nat's Treasure. By R. Leighton.

The Master of the Rebel First. By Howard Brown.

In the Misty Seas. By H. Bindloss.

The Fighting Lads of Devon. By W. M. Graydon.

The Yellow Shield. By W. Johnston.

1s. each net.

Every Girl's Library.

Uniform in style with " The Boys' Adventure" Series.

The Lady of the Forest. By L. T. Meade.

A Girl of the Fourth. By A. M. Irvine.

Margot's Secret. By Florence Bone.

A Girl in a Thousand. By Edith Kenyon.

Miss Elizabeth's Niece. By M. S. Haycraft.

The Girls Next Door. By C. Gowans Whyte.

9d. each.

Ninepenny Series of Illustrated Books.

96 pages. Crown 8vo. Illustrated. Handsome Cloth Covers.

Auntie Amy's Bird-Book. By A. M. Irvine.
Little Chris, the Castaway. By F. Spenser.
Bessie Drew, the Odd Little Girl. By Amy Manifold.
Tom and the Enemy. By Clive R. Fenn.
Birdie and her Dog. By E. C. Phillips.
Suzanne. By M. I. Hurrell.
The Young Happiness Makers. By E. Hope Lucas.
Who was the Culprit? By Jennie Chappell.
Letty; or, The Father of the Fatherless. By H. Clement.
Caravan Cruises: Five Children in a Caravan. By Phil Ludlow.
Daring and Doing. By Mrs. Crosbie-Brown.
The Children of Cherryholme. By M. S. Haycraft.
Twice Saved! By E. M. Waterworth.
Willie's Battles and How He Won Them. By E. M. Kendrew.
Into a Sunlit Harbour. By M. I. Hurrell.
Dick Lionheart. By Mary Rowles Jarvis.
A Regular Handful: or, Ruthie's Charge. By Jennie Chappell.
Little Bunch's Charge; or, True to Trust. By Nellie Cornwall.
Mina's Sacrifice; or, The Old Tambourine. By Helen Sawer.
Our Den. By E. M. Waterworth.
Only a Little Fault! By Emma Leslie.
Marjory; or, What would Jesus Do? By Laura A. Barter-Snow.
The Little Slave Girl. By Eileen Douglas.
Out of the Straight. By Noel Hope.
Bob and Bob's Baby. By Mary E. Lester.
Grandmother's Child. By Annie S. Swan.
The Little Captain: A Temperance Tale. By Lynde Palmer.
Love's Golden Key. By Mary E. Lester.
Secrets of the Sea. By Cicely Fulcher.
For Lucy's Sake. By Annie S. Swan.
How Paul's Penny became a Pound. By Mrs. Bowen.
How Peter's Pound became a Penny. By the same Author.

9d. each (*continued*).

NINEPENNY SERIES OF ILLUSTRATED BOOKS (*continued*).

A Sailor's Lass. By Emma Leslie.

Robin's Golden Deed. By Ruby Lynn.

Dorothy's Trust. By Adela Frances Mount.

His Majesty's Beggars. By Mary E. Ropes.

Lost Muriel; or, A Little Girl's Influence. By C. J. A. Oppermann.

Grannie's Treasures: and how they helped her. By L. E. Tiddeman.

The Babes in the Basket; or, Daph and Her Charge.

Cripple George; or, God has a Plan for Every Man. A Temperance Story. By John W. Kneeshaw.

How a Farthing Made a Fortune; or, Honesty is the Best Policy. By Mrs. C. E. Bowen.

Rob and I; or, By Courage and Faith. By C. A. Mercer.

Frank Burleigh : or, Chosen to be a Soldier. By Lydia Phillips.

Kibbie & Co. By Jennie Chappell.

Brave Bertie. By Edith C. Kenyon.

Marjorie's Enemy : A Story of the Civil War of 1644. By Mrs. Adams.

Lady Betty's Twins. By E. M. Waterworth.

A Venturesome Voyage. By F. Scarlett Potter.

Faithful Friends. By C. A. Mercer.

Only Roy. By E. M. Waterworth and Jennie Chappell.

Aunt Armstrong's Money. By Jennie Chappell.

Cared For; or, The Orphan Wanderers. By Mrs. C. E. Bowen.

A Flight with the Swallows. By Emma Marshall.

The Five Cousins. By Emma Leslie.

John Blessington's Enemy : A Story of Life in South Africa. By E. Harcourt Burrage.

6d. each.

Devotional Classics.

A New Series of Devotional Books by Standard Authors. Well printed on good paper. Size 6¼ by 4¼ inches. Beautifully bound in Cloth Boards, 6d. each, net ; Leather, 1s. 6d. each, net. (Not illustrated).

The Imitation of Christ. By Thomas á Kempis.

The Holy War. By John Bunyan.

New Series of Sixpenny Picture Books.

Crown 4to. With Coloured Frontispiece and many other Illustrations. Handsomely bound in Paper Boards, with cover printed in ten colours.

Little Sunbeam. By Auntie Ethel.

Fun and Frolic. By Aunt Ruth.

Little Bright Eyes' Picture Book. By Uncle Maurice.

My Picture Book. By Aunt Ethel.

Little Betty Blue ! By Uncle Maurice.

Buttercup's Picture Book. By Aunt Ethel.

Ride-a-Cock-Horse ! By Aunt Ruth.

Dolly Dimple's Picture Book. By Aunt Ethel.

Little Snowdrop's Bible Picture Book. By J. Dew.

Sweet Stories Retold. A Bible Picture Book. By J. Dew.

My Bible Picture Book ⎫
Sweet Stories of Old ⎪ Four Bible Picture Books with
The Good Shepherd ⎬ coloured illustrations.
Friends of Jesus ⎭

6d. each *(continued)*.

The "Red Dave" Series.

*New and Enlarged Edition.   Handsomely bound in Cloth Boards.
Well Illustrated.*

ONLY A GIRL! By Dorothea Moore.

THE MAN OF THE FAMILY. By JENNIE CHAPPELL.

QUITS! A Story of a Schoolboy Feud. By Maurice Partridge.

SUSIE'S SACRIFICE; or, A Fair Inheritance. By B. H. M. Walker.

"BE PREPARED!" By C. F. Argyll-Saxby.

A DOUBLE VICTORY. The Story of a Knight Errant. By Maurice Partridge.

MINNIE'S BIRTHDAY STORY; or, What the Brook Said. By Mrs. Bowen.

ELSIE'S SACRIFICE. By Nora C. Usher.

TIMFY SIKES: Gentleman. By Kent Carr.

GREYPAWS: The Astonishing Adventures of a Field Mouse. By Paul Creswick.

THE SQUIRE'S YOUNG FOLK. By Eleanora H. Stooke.

THE CHRISTMAS CHILDREN: A Story of the Marshes. By Dorothea Moore.

THE LITTLE WOODMAN AND HIS Dog Cæsar. By Mrs. Sherwood.

BRAVE TOVIAK. By Argyll-Saxby.

THE ADVENTURES OF PHYLLIS. By Mabel Bowler.

A PLUCKY CHAP. By Louie Slade.

FARTHING DIPS; or What can I do? By J. S. Woodhouse.

WHERE A QUEEN ONCE DWELT By Jetta Vogel.

BUY YOUR OWN CHERRIES.

LEFT IN CHARGE, and other Stories.

TWO LITTLE GIRLS AND WHAT They did.

THE ISLAND HOME.

CHRISSY'S TREASURE.

DICK AND HIS DONKEY.

COME HOME, MOTHER.

"ROAST POTATOES!" A Temperance Story By Rev. S. N. Sedgwick, M.A.

RED DAVE: or What Wilt Thou have Me to do?

KITTY KING. By Mrs. H C Knight.

MIDGE. By L. E. Tiddeman.

HIS CAPTAIN. By Constancia Sergeant.

"IN A MINUTE!" By Keith Marlow.

A LITTLE TOWN MOUSE.

A SUNDAY TRIP AND WHAT CAME of it. By E. J. Romanes.

LOST IN THE SNOW.

ALMOST LOST. By Amethyst.

JEPTHAH'S LASS. By Dorothea Moore.

WILFUL JACK. By M. I. Hurrell.

WILLIE THE WAIF. By Minie Herbert.

LITTLE TIM AND HIS PICTURE. By Beatrice Way.

3d. each.

The Young Folk's Library.

With Coloured Frontispiece.   64 pages, well Illustrated.   Handsome covers.

LITTLE JACK THRUSH.

A LITTLE BOY'S TOYS.

THE PEARLY GATES.

SYBIL.

A BRIGHT IDEA.

THE LITTLE WOODMAN.

RONALD'S REASON.

THE CHURCH MOUSE.

Paternoster Series of Popular Stories.

An entirely New Series of Books, Medium 8vo. in size, 32 pages, fully Illustrated. Cover daintily printed in two Colours, 1d. each.   Titles as follows :

JOHN PLOUGHMAN'S TALK. (Part I.) By C. H. Spurgeon.

JOHN PLOUGHMAN'S TALK. (Part II.) By C. H. Spurgeon.

THE LAMP IN THE WINDOW. By F. Bone.

ROBERT MUSGRAVE'S ADVENTURE. By Deborah Alcock.

FIDDY SCRAGGS; or, A Clumsy Foot may Tread True. By A. Buckland.

HAROLD; or, Two Died for Me. By Laura Barter-Snow.

"NOODLE!" From Barrack Room to Mission Field. By S. E. Burrow.

TWO LITTLE GIRLS AND WHAT they Did. By T. S. Arthur.

THE LITTLE CAPTAIN. By Lynde Palmer.

TRUE STORIES OF BRAVE DEEDS. By Mabel Bowler.

ALICE IN WONDERLAND.

THE DAIRYMAN'S DAUGHTER.

ROBIN'S GOLDEN DEED. By Ruby Lynn.

THE BASKET OF FLOWERS.

BUY YOUR OWN CHERRIES. By John Kirton.

THE GIPSY QUEEN. By Emma Leslie.

A CANDLE LIGHTED BY THE LORD. By Mrs. Ross.

GRANDMOTHER'S CHILD. By Annie S. Swan.

THE BABES IN THE BASKET; or, Daph and her Charge.

THE LITTLE PRINCESS OF TOWER Hill. By L. T. Meade.

THROUGH SORROW AND JOY. By M. A. R.

THE LITTLE WOODMAN AND HIS Dog Cæsar. By Mrs. Sherwood.

DICK AND HIS DONKEY. By Mrs. Bowen.

THE LIGHT OF THE GOSPEL.

THE BRITISH WORKMAN
AND HOME MONTHLY.
A Unique Publication.

One Penny Monthly.
1s. 6d. per annum post free.

THE RT. HON. THOMAS BURT, P.C., M.P., says:—"I should like to see THE BRITISH WORKMAN in the home of every working man; it certainly deserves to be." "A wonderful pennyworth."—C K. S. in "*The Sphere.*"

THE FAMILY FRIEND: An illustrated Magazine for every home

One Penny Monthly; 1s. 6d. per annum, post free anywhere.

THE FAMILY FRIEND has published some of the best work of ANNIE S. SWAN, SILAS K. HOCKING, LILLIAS CAMPBELL DAVIDSON, KATHARINE TYNAN, MORICE GERARD, E. EVERETT-GREEN, SCOTT GRAHAM, etc. It is the mother's companion and the growing girl's delight. No home is complete without it.

The King of Papers for all Boys and Girls.

THE CHILDREN'S FRIEND.

One Penny Monthly.
1s. 8d. per annum, post free anywhere.

"*The Children's Friend* is 'ripping.'"—YORK. "*The Children's Friend* stands supreme."—SCOTLAND. "Every bit is worth reading."—CANADA. "I love *The Children's Friend.*"—JAMAICA.

THE INFANTS' MAGAZINE.

One Penny Monthly.

No other periodical can be compared with THE INFANTS' MAGAZINE for freshness, brightness, and interest. SPLENDID COLOURED PLATE WITH EACH ISSUE. Easy Painting and Drawing Competitions. Widely adopted as a "First Reader." 1s. 6d. per annum, post free anywhere.

SUNSHINE.

One Penny Monthly.
1s. 6d. per annum post free.

A treasure-house of good things for boys and girls. In addition to a high-class serial story, there are heaps of other attractive features. Beautifully Illustrated.

THE BAND OF HOPE REVIEW.

½d. Monthly.

The Leading Temperance Periodical for the Young, containing Serial and Short Stories, Concerted Recitations, Prize Competitions, etc. Should be in the hands of all Band of Hope Officers and Members. 1s. per annum, post free anywhere.

These Magazines are published in bound Annual Volumes, from 1s. to 2s. 6d.

Free Specimen Copies sent to any address in the World on receipt of postcard.

S. W. PARTRIDGE & CO., Ltd., 21 & 22, Old Bailey, London. E.C.